days like this

danielle ellison

BOOKISH GROUP PRESS

First Edition: June 2015

Days Like This/ by Danielle Ellison

1. Fiction 2. Romance 3. Coming of Age

Summary: A young woman returns to her hometown to care for her bipolar mother and must face the secrets she's been running from and the boy she once loved.

Cover design by Jenny Perinovic

Interior layout and formatting by Jenny Perinovic

Editing by Sarah Henning

ISBN 978-0-9962205-0-7 (paperback)

to mom, for letting me go my own way.

1.

Cassie

ON THE PRETTIEST DAYS, when the sun was high in the sky, Mom pulled me out of school and drove us down the coast. On those days she would put the top down on the black convertible, and we'd fly.

This was a good day for flying.

I felt it in the air as soon as I'd woken up. The energy as the weather changed so it was the last bit of one thing, or the first hint of another. I couldn't sit in biology class, not with birds flying around in the sun on the first beautiful day of April. Life was happening outside while we studied it inside, and I wanted to be part of it. Even though I was hundreds of miles away from the ocean, I wanted to feel like I wasn't.

I rolled the windows all the way down as I drove ten over the speed limit up to Ogden Dunes Beach. My cell vibrated in the cup holder. I picked it up—Rohan—and then threw it back down. June probably told him I left in the middle of biology, so he decided to check up on me. Rohan didn't get it. He didn't understand me.

"Sweet Emotion" came on the radio, and I turned it up, let the beats overpower the wind. I hung my hand out the window and held it tight against the force. Then, I pressed harder so my hand wouldn't move. Resistance was the key. If I fought it, if I didn't give up, then I could fight anything.

Aerosmith blared around me, and I let myself wish Mom was here. This was her song, her whole playlist. I should've stopped listening to it, because every time I did, it was a reminder of what I'd been running from, but the woman knew music. Listening to her songs didn't mean I was destined to be like her, did it?

On the pretty days when we'd drive, she put the car on cruise and I'd slide into her seat, like sliding into her shoes. It was easy and exciting as I'd steered us along the empty roads. Mom would stand up in the seat next to me. I'd watched her, studied her movements and the delicate way she did everything. I'd wanted to be just like her. She laughed into the wind and threw her hat out of the car; it was gone before I could catch a glimpse of it in the rearview mirror.

"This, Cassie, this is living," she'd said. And she'd laughed this carefree laugh, like nothing could touch us.

I remember it so clearly. Her dark curls flickering in the wind, blue eyes sparkling. Head back, arms out, eyes closed—it was as if she'd let go. In the mirror, her face had looked joyful.

But that day, like so many before and after it, was all a trick. There were no pretty days with us, no peace, only days when she wasn't as sick. Only days where I could let myself block out what had happened before, or what would happen tomorrow. There were only moments of happiness before moments of heartache when I woke up and she'd be lost somewhere inside her head. She wouldn't be the mom I needed, and I'd be left alone, waiting for another pretty day.

Mid-chorus, my hand buckled against the wind; I shook it out and let it rest on the window frame. So much for resistance. Maybe it really was futile.

I left home for a lot of reasons I still didn't know how to say, but one of them was Mom. I didn't want to be anything like her, yet every single thing I did reminded me of her. Like spending today at the beach instead of being responsible Cassie. Maybe I couldn't escape the future after all and I would end up being another version of her.

But this was just a day for me. It wasn't a high before or after a low; it wasn't the best moment before the worst or a fleeting day of happiness in an endless string of sadness. Tomorrow, I'd wake up at home and still be me. I wouldn't be so low I couldn't get up, so depressed I couldn't even remember my own name. I wouldn't be a number, a statistic, or another girl with a disease.

Not yet, anyway.

I turned up the radio before the last chorus, and sang so loud I didn't have to think anymore.

2.

Graham

EVERY MORNING JOYCE Harlen waved at me from her front porch when I came home from my run. She always had a cup of coffee and some old record playing out of her open windows. Usually, she had two mugs in case I had time to sit with her and, sometimes, when she seemed lonely, I would. I could almost read it on her face, the loneliness, and she was so much like Cass in those moments it nearly killed me. Today looked like one of those days, so I stopped.

"Coffee, Graham?" she asked me.

"I'd love some coffee, Mrs. H," I said. I didn't really want coffee—I hated that stuff—but her eyes lit up when she poured it and motioned to the seat beside her. I sat, slowly, and noticed once again she left the seat across from her empty. The seat that was for Cassie. It was as if nothing was different for her: I was still the boy next door in love with her daughter and any second she would bounce out of that door and sit next to us.

She wouldn't. She'd left.

And I hated sitting and pretending that things

were the same when they weren't. Cassie wasn't part of my life anymore, never would be, but her mother was this constant reminder. I wanted to ignore her, but when she had that look on her face, and with her being bipolar and her daughter off in Indiana, I don't know. It made me feel heartless.

I should've left this town like Cass did, and then maybe I wouldn't have to be reminded every single day that I wasn't good enough.

Mrs. H handed me a mug. I took an obligatory sip. Four sips were usually all I could manage to swallow, and it tended to equal the amount of time we could sit here before she mentioned Cass. I wasn't sure which was worse. Cass's name was a shot to the chest every single time. It's not every day your fiancée leaves in the middle of the night with no reasons why.

"How's it going, Mrs. H?" I asked.

"The same as always, Graham. Not much excitement in my life, I must say, not like when I was younger," she said. When she was younger, she was a groupie. Technically, she was a manager, but the way she painted her life, all travelling and bands and pot in the seventies, she was a groupie.

"I love this song!" she yelled, slapping her hand on the little table. Her eyes were bright, as if some kind of fog passed her for only a moment. She sang along to the opening verse and then stopped. "Did Cassie ever tell you about this song?"

Cass never told me a lot of things, but this story I knew. I could even picture the way Cass would recite it in such great detail as if she had been there. Her nose crinkled up, her blue eyes sparkled as she whisked everyone away. She had a way of doing that, of making people forget that they were only hearing a story instead of living something real. But with Cass, nobody cared.

What the hell am I doing here?

"This song was the song that was playing the first time I kissed him. He was handsome—a lot like you are now," Mrs. H said. "Richard was standing across the room and the crowd seemed to part when Stevie started singing this song. Our eyes met, and that was the end."

Stevie Nicks. The gateway singer in the Harlen women's souls. Even a song like "Angel," that always seemed sad to me, brought joy to them. Cass loved Stevie Nicks the same way, with this absolute assurance that she could never be wrong about the choice. She'd loved me that way once, too. She could make me lose control with a look, make me feel like I was flying with a touch, and stop my heart with a kiss. That was the one thing I knew was true, but then she left, and even Stevie couldn't fix that.

"I should go," I said. All of this was a little too much for one morning. Her smile disappeared. I took two steps before glancing back at her. Mrs. H was staring into her house through the open window.

"Graham, do you still want to go to school for that construction thing?"

I nodded. "Architecture, yeah."

I did the construction thing, too. I'd been working with the local hardware store for odd jobs for half a year now. It started out with me helping out around Mrs. H's house. A pipe, a broken window, and then everyone started calling me. It wasn't my dream, which was architecture school, but it was money in the bank. Money that would hopefully send me to Rice University in the fall. But I still didn't know. My dreams had been wait-listed.

"Can you knock down this wall?" She pointed

through the window. Really? Those damn Harlen women. Just when I told myself I was out, they lured me back in.

I went back up the stairs and followed her direction to the wall next to the fireplace. I shook my head. That fireplace was security for the whole wall. Knocking it down would be a lot of trouble, and fixing it even more.

"Why do you want to knock it down?" I asked.

She smiled, a hand fluttering out into the air. "A big window! So I can see into the backyard."

"How big?" I asked. We could put in a window, for sure.

"The whole wall! Windows are supposed to be big, not tiny. This house doesn't have enough windows. Cassie said it always felt too small."

Sounded like something she'd say. Cassie thought this town was too small, too. This house, this town, her life. "Sorry, Mrs. H. I can't take out that whole wall for a window."

"But it's crowded."

"The fireplace is there. Pick a new wall and then maybe," I said. She shook her head slowly, not looking away. Shit. Now I've upset her. I rested a hand on her shoulder. "You okay? You taking your meds, Mrs. H?"

She shook me off. "Graham Tucker, you can't ask a woman about her meds."

I held up my hands, because if Mrs. H had been Cassie there'd be a second before I had something thrown at my head. "I'm only making sure, ma'am."

Mrs. H crossed her arms, and the bangles on her wrist jangled. "Nurse Debbie comes by every afternoon and I take my meds then. Every day."

"Okay," I said. For some reason it felt like a lie. I knew enough about Harlen women to tell that, too. "I should get to work."

She didn't pay attention to me—her eyes were on that wall and when I crossed into my yard from hers, something felt off. I couldn't figure it out, but Cass used to get that way sometimes. I would say something she didn't like and she'd shut me out. She was so determined to be right that nothing else mattered except proving that thing could exist.

Stop it.

My life no longer revolved around Cass anymore, but somehow her mother was still part of mine. The woman had no one, except a daughter hundreds of miles away doing God knows what. I didn't care what she did, and in the last eleven months, she'd made it crystal clear she didn't care what I did. Or about me at all. I had to step away from Mrs. H, because being around her meant being around Cass...even if it was only stories. Cass in stories was almost as dangerous as Cass in real life. Even surrounded by her ghost I knew that. In real life or in stories, I knew one thing for sure: Cassidee Nicks Harlen broke my heart once. She would never be allowed to do it again.

3.

Cassie

I HUGGED MY knees toward my chest. Even though it was a sunny day, it was still April in Indiana. Graham and I used to sneak off to the ocean all year round, especially after one of Mom's bad days, when I was stressed out. It was never this cold at home, but sometimes it was too cold for a rational person to sit next to the water. We didn't let it stop us. Graham would always wrap his arms around me and kiss my neck, and we'd stay that way next to the ocean until the coldness seemed to seep through my skin. Then he'd guide me to the car or the quiet place under the pier and tell me I was beautiful while his hands warmed and explored my body and made me forget I'd even been cold. Made me forget everything that wasn't him.

No thinking about Graham.

I couldn't let myself go back to those memories, or I'd never be happy without him.

My eyes scanned the shore of the lake, which was scattered with people. A boy and his mom were closest to me. He was three or four, running through the sand in steps that were too wide to keep him balanced. The woman trailed after him and rested a hand on her pregnant belly. They lingered at the cusp of the tide, and he reached for her as the waves washed over his feet.

The last time I came here I was with Rohan. I failed a test that day, which wasn't a big deal, but it felt like the world was ending. It made me cry more. The crying reminded me of Mom, of times when every small moment was really a large one. And of Graham, and the look on his face each time I disappointed him, when I made him leave me here, and that made it worse. My emotions had been out of control when Rohan found me in bed. He'd stroked my cheek with his slightly calloused fingertips, curled his body next to mine. The warmth of him had seeped through my sheets, but it was nothing like Graham's warmth or Graham's hands or even Graham's memory.

I never told Rohan why I was upset; I couldn't because he didn't know about Mom, but he'd carried me out of the bed and into the car and up here. I still hadn't told him or anyone else. Indiana made me someone new, someone without a bipolar mother, someone not at risk. I'd given up everything, including Graham, to be that person, but I wasn't sure who this new Cassie was without those things.

The boy squealed, stuck somewhere between excitement and laughter. The water crawled up to his ankles and he jumped in it, making a splash and a louder laugh. The sound made me smile.

I grabbed my notebook, writing down notes and words to the rhythms around me.

Sandcastles, snowmen, houses of cards // everything falls apart // just like you // just like me // and the life that couldn't be // things I can never get back // things I can never be // just like you // just like me // and the life that will never be

Every piece of life had music in it; we only had to find it. Writing music, writing life, helped me focus on the important moments. The ones that needed to be felt and captured and remembered. That was all music was: moments frozen into songs. I heard the songs as if they were really playing around me—and sometimes, lately, I'd been hearing the ones I was trying to forget.

My phone vibrated on my leg; it was June, and I sighed before answering it.

"Cassidee Fucking Harlen, where are you? Rohan is freaking out."

"I had to get away. Tell Rohan I'm fine."

June inhaled on the line. I almost saw her in my head as she paced outside Jason's dorm, bright red and pink hair a mess because June "doesn't do Monday mornings" and chain smoking even though she'd quit last week. And two weeks before that.

"You sure you're not having a meltdown or anything? If you're under emotional distress, I can drag Jason's ass out of bed and we can come save you. We even have a white stallion."

Jason's Mustang. We dubbed it Stallion after the homecoming parade, when Rohan and I were new and Jason was newer and would do anything to be in with June. Most people would do anything to be in with June.

"But do you have a cape? And a sword?"

She paused, breathing in and out on the line. She was definitely smoking. "Actually, yes."

"Do I want to know?"

"Probably not," June said. Her voice practically smiled across the phone. "You're sure this isn't a cry for help?"

"Yes," I said. If she knew about my mom then what

would she think? Or about Graham?

"Great, then call your boyfriend, doll. I'm going back to bed."

I glanced at my watch. 11:10 a.m. "Don't you have psych in twenty minutes? I think you should go to class instead of to sleep."

"Who said I was sleeping? Jason has a cape, and I only need ten minutes for what I have in mind."

"Gross."

"Don't be jealous. I will totally have Jason give the cape to Rohan. I know how you have a thing for superheroes," she said with a laugh before she hung up.

I'd met Rohan at a party where he was dressed as some Indian superhero. June dragged me with her to the frat party, thanks to her then fling with David Givens, and I ended up in the corner of the room, a lonely sexy nurse surrounded by superheroes. It was a theme—heroes—and apparently sexy nurse qualified. At least in June's eyes. I'd never talked to Rohan Patel before he said, "I think you're the only one who took this party literally." He stayed by my side all night, and then he helped me get June back to our dorm. He looked at me like I was being seen for the first time, and ran his fingers across my cheek, and kissed me like I was more than the broken girl, like I was the only girl, and spent the night.

My phone vibrated again. This time it was Rohan.

June said she talked to you. Where are you?

I was about to call.

You're okay?

Went on a drive. I'm coming back now.

Good. I want to show you something.

It's not a cape is it?

What? No.

What is it?

It's a surprise. Come back and meet me. I'll be at The Garage.

I hated surprises. But it was Rohan, so I would smile and pretend like I didn't hate them.

I stole one last glance at the lake where the boy and his mom were building a sandcastle. I wiped sand off my jeans as I rose to my feet and turned away.

Maybe theirs will stand longer than anything we tried to build.

I slammed the car door and had to crank the engine twice before the old convertible turned on. Around me, the sky turned that familiar shade of orange. It was the same shade as this tiny boutique Mom and I visited when we'd drive to the beach when I was younger. We always stopped at a little orange boutique with a name I couldn't pronounce, and we'd try on all the hats in the store. Especially the ones with lace. We jumped around and she talked to me in fake accents and told me her name was "Tallulah" and I was "Divine" and we'd laugh and laugh until the clerks grew annoyed.

Then we'd wander to a green store for ice cream, which had an open sign that blinked like someone was eating a cone. She ordered us a banana split because those were better if they were shared, and before we hit the road again, she'd go to the purple shop and buy a record. Something classic from the sixties or seventies. The kind of stuff Mom loved.

"This," she'd said, "is how music should sound."

That was her line every time we bought one, and when we arrived back home in the middle of the night, she'd play it before she put me to bed. It screeched and scratched on the record player, but it was the way music was supposed to sound. Eventually, I'd believe the same thing.

"It's pure," Mom had said.

Mom called a lot of things pure, whole and better. Especially the ocean. There was nothing like the ocean for us. I always thought I could keep her focused on the pretty days and she'd be okay, we'd be okay, and it would be enough, but I'd fail. I always failed.

☙ ❦ ❧

THE SKY WAS dark when I arrived at The Garage, and the sound of drums leaked out into the cool April air. I stopped right outside the heavy iron door and listened to Vinyl Drive practice. They were getting good, that was for sure. Two months ago, they landed a manager. They'd been working on a demo ever since. Rohan wasn't ready to admit the band was more than a pastime. He still planned to get his degree in engineering and go on to do something to use all his brains and make lots of money so his family could be proud. It was a standard that all three of his older siblings achieved (doctor, NASA technician, chiropractor). Music meant something more to him. Something more than a hobby, more than science, and maybe even more than his parents' approval.

It was that for me too, and it definitely connected us in a way that I hadn't felt with Graham. But where Rohan created his own music, I survived on everyone else's. He heard me once when we were driving in the car, and he stopped singing mid-song so he could listen to me. Then he turned the radio down, and said that I was good. "Really good. Better than anyone I know. You should sing more."

"I don't sing," I'd said.

"Why not? This could be your path. You wanted a

major."

"Not music," I'd snapped. Because as much as I loved it—listening to it, writing it, breathing it—that was always more Mom's thing. She was the one who'd been in the music industry, manager to some really famous bands back before I was born. She lived music, and I knew that passion flowed through my veins, but embracing it meant embracing everything that she was. I didn't want that. I didn't want one more part of me to be shaped by someone else.

Rohan struck the last chord; my ears rang in the silence. He found me immediately, his hungry eyes taking me in. The smile that danced in his gaze made all the worries melt away. He made me feel without saying anything.

Levi, the drummer, started rambling about their meeting next week, the last chance to make sure they had established a sound. A song that was a hit maker. It was a big deal for the band. Rohan commented on it, and in a quick movement, jumped off stage and pressed his lips to mine.

I knew everyone was watching, but my body didn't care nearly as much as my brain. Rohan pulled me in closer. His hand trailed the line of my waist where my shirt rose, and I leaned in, pressing our hips together. His thumb was rough against my stomach, sending chills up my spine. Vaguely, I heard the guys catcalling around us. Rohan must have heard them too, because he pulled away and stared over my shoulder. There was a noise, as the rest of the band started moving behind me.

"What's going on?" I asked.

"Can't a guy kiss his girl?"

I nodded. "You wanted to show me something?"

A smile broke out on his face. "This way."

He led me through the door beside the back of the stage and the guys yelled something. Rohan flipped them off, and then I was surrounded by darkness. It was so dark I couldn't tell if my eyes were open or shut. Warmth spread across my neck as Rohan said in my ear, "This is the moment, Cassie."

His heart raced against my back, and the feeling of him so close to me made my breath hitch. Between his hands around my waist and his breath on my neck, my body melded into his. My heart pounded too, trying to keep up with his, anxious from this surprise and from his fingers on my skin. Every part of me responded to Rohan when he touched me, from my head to my stomach to my toes. It was a feeling I still wasn't used to.

With Graham it was different. With Graham, my whole being responded. Just by a look across a room or a word. And God, a touch was like fire exploding all over my skin. I didn't have that with Rohan. What Rohan and I had was only physical, what Graham and I had was everything—multiplied by a hundred, plus soaring.

Thinking about what I left hurt. If I had stayed, maybe we'd be married right now, going to school together and I'd be really seen, really known. But I hadn't stayed. He'd put a ring on my finger, but Mom's secret about my dad leaving freaked me out, so I left. I couldn't go back to that. It was gone. I had made sure of that.

Someday I hoped I would be able to apologize.

"What's going on?" I asked again, maneuvering my body away from Rohan.

Rohan dropped his hands and for the first time it felt cold. The lights came on and Rohan smiled, arms out. A grungy, faded, white RV was parked in front of us. "What do you think?"

"What is it?"

His smile dropped. "For this summer. You, me, traveling across the country."

"What?"

"It's what you said you wanted. To travel. It needs some work but nothing we can't fix."

"You can't do that, Rohan." He gave me a look like I killed his pet turtle. The same one Graham had when I'd actually killed his in middle school. *Stop thinking about Graham.* "What about summer classes? You can't blow it off."

Rohan shrugged. "I thought it was me and you, Cass."

I froze. He'd never, ever called me that. That wasn't a name he could use. Only Graham had ever called me that. Letting Rohan call me that was wrong because it wasn't his, and I didn't want it to be. It would never be anyone else's. I shook my head. "I can't go with you all summer."

Rohan grabbed my hand and guided me toward him. His scent wrapped around me as his lips grazed my neck. I was not a weak girl; this wouldn't work, but I didn't move away.

"Think about it," he said. His voice was low and in between words he kissed my neck. "Please. For me."

His hand trailed up the bottom of my shirt, warm against my skin and somehow I said, "I will." There was a smile on his face, and then his lips crashed against mine, a force so strong it pushed me against the dirty RV. His fingertips gave me goosebumps as they found any place they could touch while he pulled off my shirt. We stumbled backward, and I shivered as Rohan pressed me into the side of that RV, my back flush against cool steel, my lips on his, and my mind drifting to another boy. I felt a little guilty about each thought even though I knew the relationships weren't the same.

When Rohan looked at me, he didn't see the girl I used to be; he saw the sexy nurse. It was scary in a way completely different from Graham. Rohan didn't have the history with me that Graham had, and maybe I needed to be seen a different way. To be seen by someone who didn't know everything about me. He knew the Cassie I presented to him, a girl who dreamed and listened to his punk rock pop crap; not the one scared of never finding her own way.

I liked him, but a whole summer? It would never last a whole summer. The sex wouldn't be enough to glue us. He'd get bored, or I would get scared, and it would be done. I'd been scared before. I was scared when I left Graham, even more scared when I let him walk away, but what we had was real. Forever, even when I'd walked away.

Rohan and I weren't forever. We were a flame. From the second we met, there was something that burned hot and fast and bright. But it wouldn't last. He didn't know me. Only one person ever got that close to me, and I broke him. It wouldn't happen again. Rohan and I had lips and bodies and nights, but deep down I missed the thing I'd let go. I let it go for the right reasons, but wanted it back for the other ones.

4.

Graham

CLYDE'S BAR WAS packed at seven on Tuesday night, but Lou was working, so it wasn't a surprise. He was the only bartender in the surrounding cities who didn't ID. Molly laughed next to me, and her hand rested on my thigh. She flipped her blonde hair over her shoulder. Each time she did it I smelled her shampoo. Lilacs or some shit. Girls always smelled like flowers or fruits or spice. It was part of their secret powers.

Molly knew how to use all hers.

The guys from the bar couldn't stop staring at her. Her legs, her chest—everything really. James, my late-twenty-something boss, was staring a little too much, so I kicked him under the table. He shrugged.

"We should go, Michael," Molly said. I hated my first name, but Cass was the one who started getting everyone to call me by my middle name. When she left, I wanted to be "Michael." "Graham" always had Cassie. "Michael" made it feel less like she was missing. At least, sometimes.

"We have that thing," Molly added when I didn't move.

I took a swig of my beer. "What thing?"

She batted her eyelashes, rubbed her hand across the crotch of my jeans, and leaned in to my ear. "The thing that involves you and me being naked."

I spit out my beer and she smiled, like some innocent little angel. But she was a devil under her southern girl charm.

Cass would never have said something like that to me. They were completely opposite in every way. I think that was why I liked Molly so much. She surprised me. By day she was a do-gooder, a nursing student holding people's hands while they died, solid and driven. By night she was someone who lived every second of life.

"We have to go," I said, helping Molly off her stool.

"See you tomorrow," James said, nodding toward me. I'd been helping James at a residential construction site. Tomorrow, it would be done. Building houses was a science and an art and a miracle at once. Construction was a lot like architecture, and even though I hadn't designed that house, I still had pride in it. Nothing was there a few months ago, and now there was a house. There would be a family. And it was all because of us.

"Sure thing."

"You bring the coffee in the morning, Mikey!" James yelled after us.

⚬✲⚬

WE WERE OUTSIDE Molly's apartment about six minutes later. That was the nice thing about a small town—it didn't take long to get places. She smiled at me, blonde hair falling in her face, and I couldn't help

20

but smile back. Molly found me four months ago at Clyde's. I was there with two friends, Eric and Lila, who were in for Christmas break, when Molly walked right up to us and asked me to dance.

"There's no dance floor," I'd said.

"We'll make our own."

Eric had practically pushed me out of the booth into Molly. I didn't think I was ready, but they disagreed. They both went to high school with Cassie and me, and when she left I guess I won the straw that said they would be my friends and not hers. Strange how that had happened.

"Have fun," Eric had said.

"Move on," Lila'd added.

Molly had been a casual thing at first. She made me smile, made me forget, and that was something I needed after Cass. I'd found my own way in the months after she left me—architecture school, construction, friends, a plan—and then Molly. Cass leaving may have been a good thing, because before that day, I was content to follow her. Now, I made my own path. Somehow Molly fit into that, at least currently. If I was accepted into college then I didn't know, but Molly didn't seem to mind the unknown. She had her own dreams.

I wondered if Cass had found hers. That was part of why she left, at least the only part she admitted to, and I hope they were worth ending us. I hoped too that it wasn't, and she missed me every day and regretted it. It felt wrong to want both things for her, but I did.

"You ready?" Molly asked.

I didn't answer. I jumped out of the car, went around to her side, as a gentleman should, and guided her out of the seat. My mouth found hers and we walked backwards, lips not parting, until we made it to her door.

❧

THE WHOLE BLOCK was dark and quiet around me, save the sound of my engine and the hum of the streetlights. I parked outside my house and it was already after midnight. Four hours of sleep was better than zero. I slammed the door shut and walked toward the back of the house to my apartment above the garage.

Cass and I used to sneak up there when we were younger, back when we were "Cass and Graham," before I graduated and moved into it to wait for her to graduate. Before she left me with the memories of waking up without her. We'd sneak up there in the night and talk about nothing, about everything, and make out until my lips hurt. It was our place. It was where I figured out what every inch of her felt like, and where to touch her in a way that made her sigh, and how to make her body tremble with pleasure, and have her cry out my name in that way that made us both come undone.

That felt like forever ago.

I shook away the thoughts, and paused to unlock the door. That's when I smelled something burning in the air, like in the summer when every house on the block grilled out. No one grilled at midnight. This was something else. I turned around, scanning the woods for anything off. If there was a fire in the woods it would be at our houses in minutes.

Then I saw the smoke. And it wasn't coming from the woods.

Fuck.

"Mrs. H!" I yelled, and took off in a sprint toward Cassie's house. I raced over there. It felt like I wasn't moving at all, like I was running through water. I jumped over the half-broken fence between our backyards, and rounded toward the backdoor of her house. I could see the flames and the smoke thick in the air.

The door was locked so I pounded on it, calling her name. I made out the top of her head from where she was curled up in a ball on the couch. I grabbed a rock from the ground and smashed in the window on the door. Glass crackled against the tile floor, and I yelled her name as I crossed into the house. Smoke stung my eyes, a grey haze that draped over everything.

Mrs. H was sitting on the couch, and she was bawling. "It's so small in here. Too small."

Shit. The whole wall where she wanted the window was engulfed in flames. We had to get the fuck out.

"I know. Let's go outside where it's not small," I said.

I tried to get her up, but Mrs. H fought against me. Her arms thrashed in the air and I wasn't sure what the hell I was supposed to do. She wouldn't stand up. She kept throwing herself on the ground.

"I want Cassie! Where's Cassie? It's too small here, but it's bigger now. Cassie!"

I bent down and tilted her face up to mine. "Cassie isn't here. She's at my house, Mrs. H."

Her eyes widened like I was Santa. "Your house?"

"Come on, you can see her." I tried to keep my voice calm, but I knew I was really yelling. I had to get us out of there. Lying seemed like the only option. I'd seen her before like this, and it's what Cass always did. Lied to her.

Mrs. H started to stand, so I swooped her up and

carried her out of the house. We collapsed in the backyard.

I dialed 911, out of breath and tired, and beside me Mrs. H was still crying. I didn't know what to do to calm her down. So again I did what Cassie would have done and started humming while we waited. Mrs. H was still crying on the ground, legs to her chest, so I sat down beside her and watched the smoke trail up from the house.

"Sometimes," I whispered, trying to sing. Singing wasn't my thing, but I sang "Angel" the best I could. I knew the words as if it was my favorite song, but I hated that song. I would hate it forever.

Mrs. H rested her hand on my arm. "Where's Cassie?"

I didn't answer. It was hard to believe that this happened and Cassie was nowhere around. Did I miss the signs? I knew them. I learned them four years ago when Mrs. H was diagnosed as bipolar.

I'd realized something was wrong when I was twelve, and I'd found them in the snowstorm, but I'd kept it a secret. I'd been there when Cassie put Mrs. H to bed, or ran guys out of their house, or cried herself to sleep, or disappeared for days. Cassie didn't talk about it much, even to me, and I'd never pressed her. She was the type who closed up tighter and recoiled if I'd tried to force her into something. Instead, I'd been there for her. I'd signed that emergency contact form when I turned eighteen because they wouldn't let Cassie sign it yet. I did anything I could for her, and yet...

"Where's my Cassie?"

She left.

The sirens blared around us, and firefighters worked to put out the flames. A medic wrapped a blanket around Mrs. H. "Where's Cassie?" Mrs. H asked again. I didn't want to hear her name. Not when it was the one that started all of this. Not when it was her who should've been here instead of me. And especially not when that fire meant I had to fucking call her after all this time.

5.

Cassie

JUNE PLOPPED DOWN next to me and sighed dramatically. I didn't give her attention because that would mean the end of studying. The first time we met she'd made the exact same entrance, told me to smile, said I looked boy-sick, and then called me badass for being named after a rock legend when I told her my name.

"I'm June. Country legend. So we're obviously meant to be friends," she'd said, reaching her hand out for mine.

"Do you have a Johnny?" I'd asked.

June crossed her arms. "I am the Johnny. Legends don't need a counterpart."

We'd been friends ever since.

June threw an eraser at me and sighed again. I looked up at her over my sunglasses.

"Wait, you're studying, too?" she asked.

I pointed down at my textbook. "This isn't for fun, if that's what you're asking."

"What is that, anyway?" June leaned across the metal table, tilted her head sideways. "'The French

Revolution ended the age of absolute monarchy in France, but was...' Why am I already bored?"

"I don't know. It's going to start talking about the Reign of Terror and you're an expert on those," I said.

June stuck out her tongue and leaned back in her chair. "Let's get out of here."

I shook my head. "I have a test tomorrow."

June frowned and crossed her arms. She was like a kid, except she was rough around the edges, dropped f-bombs like breadcrumbs, and had more hair colors than days of the week.

"Screw tests! Finals are in a month. They shouldn't do that to us. We need to have *lives,*" she said. Then she rose to her feet and yelled, "We get to have lives!"

A few people around us clapped. She smiled and slightly bowed. June was like that. She was bright and loud, so everyone paid attention to her. She was like Mom on a pretty day, but nothing like her at the same time. This was all June and not a sickness.

"You going to eat those?" she asked, pointing to the cheese fries on my left.

"They've been sitting here for an hour," I said. "They're cold."

She shrugged and I shoved them toward her. Only June would eat nasty cold cheese fries.

"When are you going to be done?" she asked.

"Where's Jason?"

June tapped my pencil on the tabletop. "Class. Loser."

I smirked. "Class is sort of why we're all here. Why aren't you in class?"

"It's speech. I'll wear a low-cut top and get an A. Everyone knows that." It was true. But even if it wasn't, she would still get an A. Put June in the front of a room and I dare someone not to watch her or listen to her talk about string cheese. It wasn't possible. She was smart, too. I'd always thought she was one of those secret geniuses, because it was the only way to explain how a girl who never studied and barely went to class got As. That and the low-cut tops.

She shoved a fry into her mouth and scowled. "These are cold."

I shook my head and refocused on my book, even though I knew I was done. There was no focusing when June was around and needed attention.

"I'll go get them warmed. Who's working?" Then, she was gone. I turned my head toward the student center and watched June lean over the counter. José was working today, so she'd probably be back with a whole new container of fries.

"Never Going Back Again" started playing from my phone as it vibrated across the table. I picked it up; my heart pounded a little too much, and I pushed the button.

"Mom?"

There was a soft noise, the sound of someone breathing on the other end. I pressed my fingers between the crisscross patterns on the table. Mom rarely called me, and if she was calling now it meant something was wrong.

"No, Cass."

It was a whisper on the line, but I felt it as if it was a scream injected straight into my brain. I stood up from my seat, looking out over the soccer field. My heart raced along with the ball. I forced my eyes closed, and I saw him there. Like he was standing right in front of me with those deep grey eyes that saw through me, and that wavy light brown hair I used to run my hands through. He was so real, even in a whisper, that I could almost touch him through the phone.

"Graham?" My voice cracked as I said his name. My hands were sweating, heart racing, and I was sure I wouldn't be able to hold onto my phone. I hadn't spoken to Graham in almost a year. Not since he came here for me after I left North Carolina and broke his heart. Since I gave him back his ring. And now he was calling me.

"I don't mean to call like this, but—"

"Wait, you're on my mom's phone."

The only reason he would be on Mom's phone would be to get my new number. He shouldn't need that. My heart raced because I knew. I felt it as my world tilted from balanced to out of control. Graham sighed on the line, and I could almost see it, too. He had this way of responding that showed in his whole body. Every emotion—the sighing, the laughing, the anger—encompassed all of him.

"You need to come home, Cass."

Come home. See him. Really see him. The thought made my stomach jump.

"Woo! Cassie, I got fries and ice cream!" June yelled as she busted through the door. I turned my back to her. Thousands of scenarios blew through my mind. Mom was hurt or worse. All because I wasn't there. Did I call her this week? I couldn't remember.

"What—why?"

But I knew the answer. Graham Tucker and I made a pact a long time ago, long before we were ever anything more than friends. If something happened, he would be the one who called me, not some doctor. He would be there. But I needed him to say it, because I didn't want whatever it was to be true.

"She's in the hospital, Cass. You're the only one who can make decisions. You have to come. She needs you."

I swallowed. "What happened?"

Graham grew quiet and around him I could hear the familiar sounds of the psychiatric wing at St. John's. The hum of the radiator from the fifties that still hadn't been replaced because the residents were crazy, why did they care? And I could hear the nurses moving around because they talked louder there instead of in hushed voices like most places. Especially Sheila. And he was probably standing in the blue waiting room, the one that had a puzzle of a yellow cat with the missing piece in the tail. It was hundreds of miles away yet it was still in my head, still with me no matter how far away I was.

"She almost burned the house down," he said. I sucked in some air; let it fill my lungs because it was the only way I wasn't going to lose it. Graham paused, and I wondered what he was thinking. I didn't know what I was thinking. I couldn't think. He started talking faster. "Mrs. Pearson went by to check on her and saw the flames from the window. She was sitting on the couch while the fire burned in the living room, and she lost it when they saved her."

I closed my eyes, inhaled, exhaled. I tried not to think about the fact that I was talking to him after eleven months. That my mom was in trouble. I don't think I called this week; I should've. My chest was caving in. My head was spinning. What was I going to do? I couldn't drop everything. Finals and projects and—

"She needs you," Graham said. His voice was low, and I could tell that he didn't want to have this conversation with me. But he would because he had to, and because even though there were states stretched between us, he was right next to me. He was part of me.

"You promised," he added, his voice husky.

Those little words and then nothing else mattered. If anyone had said them to me, anyone, I could've not given in. I could've stalled and figured out another solution. But not him. It almost wasn't fair that he could still have this effect on me.

"I'll need a couple days." It felt like I was holding my breath underwater. Like I was waiting for someone to rescue me, or to tell me to come out now because the storm had passed. But no one would say it. No one could stop it or change it, not when I was this far under. "I'll be there," I said.

"Okay, Cass," he said. He said my old nickname, and I froze. I could remember the last time he called me that, when he proposed and we spent the weekend locked away in some cabin in the mountains before I went home and everything changed. He would whisper my name as he kissed my lips, my cheeks, my neck, my breasts, and tell me that he was the luckiest person in the world. I'd say I was luckier, and it was true. That was always true.

Graham lingered on the line, and I thought—hoped—that he'd say something else, but he didn't. I didn't blame him. Not even goodbye. We just sat there, neither of us speaking, breathing into the receiver, and listening, waiting.

Behind me June called my name, but I didn't answer. Graham's breathing disappeared. I kept the phone pressed against my ear even though he'd hung up, and told myself it would be okay. My head didn't believe me. My heart didn't either. They both knew. They knew that this moment, this feeling, was what happened right before we drowned—and that the only person who I wanted to save me could barely talk to me.

6.

Cassie

I'M LEAVING ON SATURDAY. Just say it, Cassie.

"Water?" Rohan asked, handing me a bottle over my shoulder. I took the water from his hand, and he leaned in to kiss me before he let go. This conversation wasn't one I wanted to have, but he had to know. I had to tell him. I couldn't be in another situation like I had with Graham, or carry the guilt from sending him away. I had enough of that to carry me through forever.

Rohan pressed his lips against my neck—once, twice, three times. I could only think of Graham. I hadn't been able to get his voice out of my head since his phone call, so I pulled away from Rohan and curled my legs into his couch. He slumped down by me, hand resting on my knee.

"Are you still mad about the RV? That was days ago. I told you it's fine now."

"I'm not mad," I said. I was never mad; I was uncomfortable. It was a big commitment and he didn't even know me. That's all I could think: he didn't know me.

"The guys are pitching in and we're fixing it up for the band."

"For a tour?"

Rohan smiled. "Yeah, Stan set it up. We're recording the demo in two days and Stan has a meeting with The Pitheads manager next week."

He was glowing, bouncing all over the couch. I had to smile at his smile. "You remember them, right? That 'Girl with a Tattoo' song. We saw them with Levi?"

"Right." I remembered an underground concert with sticky floors and drunk girls and something considered music that was a blend of bad techno and screaming noise. It was horrible.

"If the meeting goes well?" I asked.

"Vinyl Drive would open. Fifteen cities, three weeks. Stan thinks he can get the new stuff in front of labels in a few weeks because of the online fan base. He already has a meeting set up." They'd had a buddy shoot a video for YouTube. It went viral in less than twenty-four hours. That was how Stan found them two months ago, and that was how all this was moving so quickly. A label was huge. "Then who knows? Your boyfriend could make it."

In the six months I'd known him, I'd never heard Rohan talk like this. He was usually wrapped up in what was expected of him from his family, his professors, and himself. He'd had a five-year plan, and then the band happened, and now he was talking like this.

"Does he want to?" I asked.

He ran his fingers across the tips of my hair, and his knuckles grazed my neck. "He thinks so."

"And his parents?" I'd never met his parents, but he talked about them enough. He and his brothers were second generations in this country from Bangladesh. His grandparents started with nothing, and worked hard to build a life for their families. Rohan and his siblings were expected to make it count, to do something that mattered, and music would definitely not fit into that category. Rohan had said that much to me enough times to commit it to memory.

Rohan laughed awkwardly. "They will probably disown him. But maybe not? I don't really know yet. One step at a time."

I smiled, feeling a little relieved. If this happened for him then it would be okay. He would have something else to make him happy, something real and not me. All I had to do was tell him. All I had to do was say two words.

"Close your eyes."

I raised an eyebrow. "Last time I did that there was an RV."

"I couldn't fit an RV in here," he said.

"I'm sure you understand my apprehension." Surprises and eyes being closed didn't really work out for me. Not last time, not eleven months ago. Even June knew I hated surprises. This was more evidence that Rohan didn't really know me.

Rohan put a finger on my lips. "Trust me. Eyes closed."

With my eyes closed, everything yelled at me to tell him that I was leaving. I couldn't tune out the voices, or the longing. It couldn't be that hard to say the words to a boy I didn't love, not like I still loved Graham. I fluttered my eyes open, but Rohan pressed his mouth against mine and his hands ran down my back. I wanted to tell him, but I didn't. Instead I tried to forget. I kissed him back, and eased his shirt over his head as he took off mine. He ran his fingers across my breasts before taking off my bra, and then all my thoughts were gone.

Three seconds. Then I lost control of my own brain and my body operated on autopilot.

Five seconds. The amount of time before my back was flush with his leather couch and it gently tugged at my skin, but I didn't let it stop us.

Seven seconds. Then I didn't feel guilty; I didn't feel anything except him on top of me. I turned to dust and nerves and no words survived.

"Cass..." he whispered, his lips trailing down my stomach.

My body tensed up at the name, but Rohan didn't notice. The weight of Graham's name for me, of his voice saying it when we made love, of him on the phone before, the memory of it all came crashing back over me. It made me kiss Rohan harder.

IT WAS 2 A.M. when I woke up. "Cass" echoed off Rohan's walls, a refrain from my dreams. The name didn't belong in his room. Over and over it played, but it wasn't Rohan's voice. It was Graham's.

Rohan was asleep next to me, his long lanky body spread across the bed and through the sheets. I looked at him and expected, hoped, to feel something. Something that made me want to stay. Something more powerful than my fear of going home again to face Graham, and my mom, and my past. But there was nothing. I wanted to talk to Graham, to tell him I left because of what I found in Mom's room, that my dad was alive and he abandoned us, and how much it scared me to ruin his life the way Mom's disorder ruined mine. It was a lot of words, and part of going home meant getting to tell him, and maybe, starting over.

So I grabbed a paper off the floor and scribbled: *I'm sorry to leave like this. I wanted to tell you I was leaving, but I didn't know how. I don't think you'll miss me and you deserve someone better. Someone who has a heart to give completely and only to you.*

I read and re-read it. He deserved more, but it was good enough—my goodbye on the back of a chemistry test. It was something. I put it on my pillow, grabbed my clothes, and ran away from the name. If I could have, I would've left all the voices there in that room. I tried before to move on, but they were a haunting refrain that seemed to follow me. Hopefully, this one would stay where it belonged.

I CRAMMED THE last box into my car and forced the back door to shut. That was everything. It was 4 a.m. and I was leaving like a thief in the night, but it was better this way. No goodbyes, no awkward emotions, no questions or half-truth explanations. They would all wake up and I would be gone. Eventually, the semester would end and they would forget about me. I was doing them all a favor. I'd spent my whole life trying to keep my mom's mess a secret, and I didn't want to drag anyone else into the pit with me. I didn't want to make them carry around my burdens.

I used to think Indiana would make everything better, that I could move on and start a new life, but everything reminded me of what I left behind. I wondered about Graham, and deep down I had this twinge of a dream for us where we were at least friends. Maybe that was impossible now, maybe me leaving made it impossible, but maybe it wasn't. I knew he was angry, but I could explain. If there was an excuse good enough to forgive a fiancée leaving in the middle of the night.

I lowered myself into the driver's seat and turned on the headlights. The engine purred along with the end of a Pink Floyd song, and June's silhouette appeared in front of my car. Her arms were crossed over her chest and her hair was a mess. She looked tired. And pissed.

I could have driven away, but leaving her like that would make leaving worse. It would be the end, and I wasn't ready to let go of that yet. She was still my friend, no matter what I was hiding, so I opened the door.

"Do you realize how fucking pissed I was to call your room and have your roommate answer and tell me all your shit was gone? That you were leaving?"

"June."

She put up a hand and I recoiled. I knew better than to mess with her when she was like this. "Do you know that I—your fucking best friend—looked like an idiot in front of dumb roommate Suzie Sunshine—whom you told you were leaving before me, and I know that was a mistake because we hate her. And I had to ramble about how I 'forgot that was today'? For someone who hates surprises, you sure aren't opposed to leaving other people shocked!"

I pressed my fingers into my palm. She had a right to be upset, but I couldn't explain this to her. Suzie asked why I was packing boxes, and she lived with me so I had to tell her. I didn't think June would be this upset. "June, it's complicated."

She exhaled. "Is this because of that call the other day? You've been weird as hell since then."

I shifted, but didn't answer. Before Graham called, I was surviving. But the last few days have been me doing some kind of recon on something that I didn't know how to protect or save. I didn't even really want it.

"Did you tell Rohan?"

My eyes shot up to see June lighting a cigarette. She shook her head at me like she didn't know me and took a long drag. "You're sneaking away? Just like that?"

"I thought it would be easier," I said.

"For us or for you?"

I didn't answer because she was right. She knew that though, or she wouldn't have said it.

"Where are you going?" Her voice was low, and she crossed her arms over her chest.

"Home," I said. "The dean approved my leave."

"I thought you loved it here? You said that over and over."

"It's my mom," I said. It wasn't a lie, not like the loving it part. The only part I loved was June, but that wasn't the same.

June exhaled smoke. "Look. We all have family shit that we don't want to air out. Trust me. I get it. But you're my best friend, and you can't disappear on me."

"It's what I do," I said with a half smile, but she didn't laugh. It wasn't a joke; it's what I did to my mom, to Graham, to the whole state of North Carolina. I flipped them off and drove away in the middle of the night.

"Not this time," she said. "You don't have to tell me anything, but when I call you better answer the phone or I will come down to North Carolina and pound your ass, Harlen."

"Got it," I said, but it would be hard. Balancing old and new wasn't something I did well. June hugged me. Neither of us were the hugging type. My arms were hard at my side, surprised at her motion. I guess I could try to balance it all for her. "I should go."

June nodded as I got in the car. "What about Rohan?" She called over the engine.

"He'll be fine. I left a note."

"Classy," she snapped, taking another drag of her cigarette. June didn't act like she believed me. She didn't move from her spot as I backed out. Part of me wished she would so I could ignore the feeling in my gut that always came with leaving. June saluted the air toward me. "Be safe."

I watched her stance from the rearview mirror until she was only the speck of red from the glow of her cigarette. I slammed on the brakes so some drunk girls coming back from a party could cross in front of me. Normal college freshmen did not go home to take care of their mothers, or to face the fiancé they left behind. Normal nineteen-year-olds didn't have an ex-fiancé, but Graham and I weren't normal. We were in love. We'd always been in love.

Before I turned away from my dorm, I glanced out the mirror for June. But I was too far away, and she was already nothing but darkness and a memory.

It wasn't as sad as I imagined; I was leaving her behind, but I was also going home. To Mom and to Graham. Even though I left him once, there was still the chance that he would understand why I left. I needed that so I could move on. Whatever that meant.

7.

Graham

I HATED THE psych wing. The first time I ever came here was four years ago, after Mrs. H was officially diagnosed and Cass missed school for a week. I would bring homework and burgers from Chevy's and we would sit in the kids' bright blue waiting room and pretend all of this was normal. It still smelled the same, like nothing and lemon. I'd never been into a place that smelled so bland before.

Mrs. H looked the same as ever, and that was what I always found strange with this. She seemed so unscathed by all of it. We never knew when it was coming; I could tell she'd had a bad day after it'd happened; Cass was usually more on edge, more cautious, careful, and tired, she would be so tired. When I thought back to childhood, there were little signs I could see in Mrs. H that I didn't know to look for. A strange sparkle in her eye, an adventure with Cass, a day or two or three where Cass didn't go to school.

But for me, Mrs. H was always the same. Joyce Harlen was eccentric. With her music, her records, and her clothes from the seventies. She was the fun mom who gave all the teens in the neighborhood alcohol when they came over. She had the stories about bands, had traveled, and had a way of doing things that was all her own. She was "eccentric" the way Cassie was contagious.

Cass was full of energy and passion and everyone else had to run to catch up to her walk. Even my mom would say, "That girl is contagious." I didn't know what she meant back then, but when Cassie laughed, the whole room laughed. When Cassie was sad, everyone felt it. When she got an idea in her head, no one doubted her ability to do it. Everyone believed her. Believed her stories, her smile, believed that she had a chance to do something different.

Different. Eccentric. Contagious. Maybe they were the same thing, the normal thing, and I was the stable one who never made sense in her life. Why would she want dependable when she could have adventure?

"I can't wait for Cassie," Mrs. H said. "Can you get her some snacks? You remember her favorites?"

I nodded. Snacks. Cheetos, Oreos, peanut butter. "Sure thing." I had no intention of buying Cassie snacks.

She patted my hand. "You're a good boy, Graham. Good for my girl. You'll be together forever. I know it."

I swallowed back the emotions, fought off the words tangled in my throat. None of them could come out, not here and not now. Mrs. H wouldn't be able to handle the things I had to say. "I should go," I said, and bolted out of the room as quick as I could.

Nurse Sheila called my name while I waited for the elevator. "Here again, Mr. Tucker?" Sheila asked, putting a hand on her hip. She was a nice woman. I met her that first time when she came in and started harping on Cassie to eat food that wasn't from a vending machine. She was a staple around here. Weird to say, but her grey-streaked hair was always something familiar and comforting.

"Any word on when our girl will be here?" she asked.

I braced myself. "Tomorrow, if all goes well."

Our girl.

"You best get our girl to school before she forgets what it looks like."

"Our girl needs to get home."

"All our girl needs is someone to hold her hand through this."

Those are all things Sheila used to tell me about Cass. *Our girl.* As if we were the ones holding her up. I never told her either that "our girl" felt we were only holding her back.

I stared at Sheila as the radiator kicked on. It sounded like a car backfiring, so loud and unexpected when it rattled through all the halls and rooms. "Sorry, what?"

Sheila shook her head and waved me off. "I said I bet you and Mrs. Harlen are thrilled."

"Yeah," I said. "Thrilled." The elevator dinged and the doors opened, and I left without another thought.

8.

Cassie

I PARKED OUTSIDE my house and expected it to be different, but it wasn't. It was just my home, one that I didn't know how much I missed. My eyes drifted to Graham's house. The white flowers his mom loved lined the front yard. I helped her plant those the first month they moved in, and she explained what they were and the best way to make them grow.

Removing my notebook in my glove box, I wrote down some lyrics as they popped into my head.

The first time I saw you // in that old Beatles shirt // you were smiling at me // like you knew the secrets of the world // I was nine, sitting on my fence // in some old red boots // that didn't really fit // I said, why you here? // You said it was all new // I said it was boring // you said, that's cause you don't know you // And I-I-I knew it would be me and you // we would take on the world together // make it something new // and I-I-I saw my whole future laid out // and it was you

I've been home three minutes and Graham Tucker was already a song. I guess he always had been. Maybe he'd been the chorus in every song.

I threw the notebook back in the glove box and stepped out of my car. Home. Or whatever was left of it. Why would Mom try to burn it down? Something burrowed in my throat—nerves maybe?—and it felt like a moment before. Before I learned Mom was sick, there was always a moment at the end of a pretty day when I realized tomorrow would be different. I recognized it immediately. Fear was an old friend and it waited in the shadows, ready to grab me.

I pushed away the feeling and walked toward the door. My key fit in the door, as if nothing had changed in the last eleven months. I could smell the lingering charred scent in the breeze of the doorway. Four days later it still smelled like disaster. I had a feeling it would be a reoccurring theme.

Inside, the foyer was covered in coats and half-empty boxes of junk. Dining room with a card table and wilted flowers. Two foldout metal chairs. We only used this table to eat on, and if there were more people over other than the two of us, we'd gather chairs from all over the house or sit on the floor like Mom said they did in other cultures. There was plenty of space in the room, but the rest of the dining room was for music.

Three walls of bookcases, ceiling to floor, held our records and two record players. One was my grandma's, and her mom's before that. The other was one of the newer ones they released in high school, when the world decided vinyl was "in" again. Records filled the room, all these powerful music and lyrics from generations were crammed here together. Knowing that some things could live on had been the only thing to comfort me as a kid.

I had to put one on. I knew right where to go since we kept them all in alphabetical order. We'd spent a whole week organizing them the summer I left. Sometimes, Mom and I would get into moods and change them around by best song title, or album title, or year, or genre. But usually, knowing where to go was always the best decision. The record scratched as I turned on Billie Holiday and let "Moaning Low" play through the house. I waited until she started singing before going to face the living room.

The fireplace wasn't white brick anymore. Now, it was black. The wall around it was charred, beams and insulation showing through the burnt drywall. I stepped closer to examine it. What was she doing? This would cost a fortune to fix.

"It's probably not safe for you to touch that," a voice said behind me. I jumped, but I knew it was Graham. My heart was already pounding, and I willed it to calm down. It was early morning, but there he was. I felt him behind me, attached to me, and that was terrifying. I stepped away from the wall, but couldn't turn around. I was frozen. Hearing his voice reminded me how much I missed it, missed him, and I couldn't see him. If I did, that would be it. I would be face-to-face with the boy I loved for years, the boy I walked away from.

Graham groaned behind me, like he was stretching. He never could stand still.

"You just get here?" he asked.

"Yeah, long day," I said. It came out a whisper.

I didn't move my gaze from the wall while all the words pierced through my head. *I'm sorry. I still love you. I hope you can forgive me. I want to be friends.* I pressed my eyes shut, quickly, and inhaled.

"It's not as bad as it looks," he said. The wall, he meant. "No structural damage since they caught it in time. It's all surface level." His voice was oddly calm. Maybe that was because I didn't know I would be able to catch mine.

"Cass," he said. It felt right hearing my name from his mouth. Then his hand was on my arm. It was a gentle touch, but it set me on fire. My whole body responded to it, chills covered me and my heart jumped around in my chest. After all this time I still felt this way with him, he could still, with a touch, make my body want him. I turned around, our eyes locked, and he stopped moving. I barely breathed.

I knew he sensed our connection, too. He felt everything more than me. I always thought it was because he wanted it more, wanted me and us more than I had. I thought it was why he proposed, and it was definitely part of why I said yes. I knew at seventeen that I wanted to be with him—but some of that was influenced by how much he'd wanted me.

Graham moved his hand from my arm, but the chills didn't go away as I took him in. He was the same in all the ways that mattered. Same deep hazel eyes, but they looked at me differently. Like I was a stranger. Short light brown hair tussled, as if he'd just woken up, and this scruffy beard that made him look older, rougher, and hotter. He was in grey sweats, white t-shirt, black flip-flops. The shirt fit him a little tight around the arms; he was buffer now, like he'd been working out. He'd always wanted muscles like that, and I'm glad he did it.

He looked better without me. He looked damn good, in fact.

Graham cleared his throat, pulling his gaze from mine. "If you want it, my mom made up the guest room for you. She thought you might be more comfortable."

"She did? Why?" It came out sharper than I meant for it to. The walls were closing in around me. It was all him. Him being here, him touching me, me staying at his house. I didn't know where to put it all. It didn't fit into a category, just as we hadn't.

"I didn't tell her anything. She knows you went to school and that's all," he said. His voice was a low grumble.

"Why would you do that?"

Graham shifted on his feet and scrubbed a hand down his neck. He was nervous. I was nervous too, because I wanted to be here as much as I didn't. I wanted to stand closer to him and have him touch me again. Even something as simple as his hand on my arm, or my hand in his, or our hips pressed against each other. I wanted to feel him next to me, close as skin, and kiss him like I'd never left. I wanted to touch him.

But I couldn't. He didn't want that, or he'd be doing it now. He was over me, and that was what I told him to do. I couldn't touch him, even if I wanted to. He deserved more than that. More than a half-life with me, and a happiness I'd never give him, even if I wanted to.

"It's not something I like to advertise, Cassie," Graham said. "I told her you moved on without me and that was the end."

I shifted my gaze to my feet. That was what I told him, almost exactly that way. I said I wasn't good for him and he should move on. *"Let's both just move on."* But I didn't think I ever knew how. Not really.

"You coming over, then?" he asked.

"You still live in the back?"

He nodded. "I won't even see you. I go to work in a couple hours anyway."

I inhaled when he said that. He definitely didn't want me around. It felt like he poured cold water down my back. Reality sucked.

"Sure," I said. I'd stay there. If he didn't care then I shouldn't either. He turned back toward the front door and I took one last look around the living room. The music stopped around me, the floor creaked in that one spot between the dining room and the foyer.

"Don't worry—I put it back in the sleeve and in the right order. I know how it works," he said, opening the door.

"You remembered," I said. If he remembered that, maybe he remembered us. The good us. Before. Memories were frozen and all I had to do to repair us was unfreeze them.

"I was never the one who forgot," he said. I stepped aside in the doorway to let him exit first.

9.

Graham

I KNEW CASS WAS coming. Hell, I was the one who called her, but until she was standing there refusing to make eye contact—it was hard to believe it was true. We'd barely said two words to each other since we left her house. I didn't really know what to say to her. Well, I knew what to say to her, but I also knew I couldn't. It wasn't the time, and I wasn't an ass. She made herself pretty clear last time I saw her. God, I wished she didn't look so damn good. If she looked bad all this would be easier.

And maybe I wouldn't want to kiss her so much.

God, I wanted to kiss her.

I had to shake that off. I had a girlfriend, and Cassie was here, but it didn't change anything. I opened the door to the guest room, and turned the light on for her. In the light of the room, she was radiant. She'd always been beautiful, but today, there was something else, a sadness that rarely defined her, but now it seemed so engrained.

I knew right then what I really wanted for her: I

hoped that when she left she found the thing that made her happy. That the sadness in her eyes was only the situation, and not what she had become. I cared too much about her to see her swallowed in sadness.

"This looks nice," Cassie said. "Very different."

When I met her gaze, I recognized a glimmer of the girl I used to love. What did she see in this room? The brown and blue paint that used to cover it? The pictures of her and me that used to plaster the walls? The Clash poster that hung on the closet door? The basketball trophies? The first time we fumbled our way through sex when we were sixteen on that very bed? We'd improved a lot since that first time. The last time I made her yell my name over and over, and it always felt awesome to be the one to make her come. I had everything I could ever want, and all of it was her, especially in that last moment we had together. I felt like a king as she called my name as I moved inside her, and I caught a glint of my diamond on her finger. I'd thought in that moment that she'd be mine forever in every way possible. That'd we have this for the rest of our lives. The memory was as vivid as if it had been yesterday, even though it'd been months.

I cleared my throat. *Stop thinking about that.* "A lot has changed."

Cassie nodded, and bit down on the side of her cheek. That used to bug me so much, because it always meant she was uncomfortable. I didn't like being the one she was uncomfortable around. "Want some water or something?" I asked.

"No, thanks."

I couldn't stop staring at her. Her hair was short now, shorter than ever, and darker too. So dark it made her eyes a bright blue. She'd always worn it long, past her shoulders, and I used to love the way it'd be a tangled mess after sex, and how we'd lie in bed after and she'd twist it around her finger like she was nervous to look at me.

Stop staring at her, Tucker. Leave.

"I guess you're good then. Night."

"Goodnight," she said. Her voice was low, and she bit the side of her cheek again. Part of me wanted to ask her what was wrong, but I knew the answer. I knew it was me, it was here, it was all the things she hated in one place. The sad part was I used to be the one thing that made her happy. Or so I'd thought.

"Graham," she called. I inhaled and turned back to face her. Her hair was new, but she stood in that room like she fit there. Even though the paint was different and we were different and so much time had passed, she still belonged there. And it was damn annoying because it was the one place she didn't want to belong. "Thank you."

I waved her off. "The room was all Mom."

She shook her head slightly. "For my mom. For being here to help. For the call."

The only thing I could think of to say was "someone had to do it" but I didn't want to see her face when I said it. So, I nodded and walked out the back door.

⌒⌒⌒

I WAS AFTER orange juice. It was a few minutes past 7 a.m. and I was going to go into the kitchen, get the juice, and get out. But Mom was already up and behind the stove. A stack of pancakes was forming beside her, and I thought twice about going inside. If she saw me, she would plan for me to stay, too. I couldn't eat pancakes across from Cass and my mom and pretend everything was normal when it wasn't. Mom probably wanted me to, especially since Dad left this morning for Japan, but I couldn't. I'd have to tell her the truth eventually, I guessed, about why we weren't together.

"Graham, you can come inside," she yelled out the window.

"I only need orange juice," I said, closing the door behind me.

Mom huffed. "I'm making pancakes."

"I see that."

"Blackberry—those were always Cassie's favorite, remember?"

I'd never forget. Cass stayed over once when I was seventeen, and my parents were in New York City visiting my brother, Timothy; we woke up to a batch of blackberry pancakes and my parents sitting at the table. "I made your favorite, Cassie," Mom had said. Cassie had on my clothes and hair all over the place. A whole weekend of teenage drinking and sex will do that. I thought for sure they would say something else, and I already had three escape routes planned in my head, but they didn't. Instead, Cassie'd said, "Thank you," and we all ate breakfast like it was the most normal thing in the world. Later, I'd heard all about having her over here, and using protection, and pregnancy—the whole thing.

"I remember, Mom," I said. She laughed a little, but didn't turn around. I grabbed the orange juice out of the fridge. "I can't stay though."

"Why not?"

"Have to go to the site."

"I thought they finished up the day of the fire?"

Crap. "About that fire—Cassie doesn't know."

"Doesn't know what?"

I took a sip of the juice but Mom stared me down. "That it was me who saved Mrs. H. I told her Mrs. Pearson called 911."

Mom put her hand on her hip, looked at me like I was insane, and held her spatula in the air with the other hand. "You lied to her?"

"I didn't want her to know it was me," I said, sitting down.

Mom shook her head. She wouldn't understand why, not if I didn't tell her the truth. The skillet sizzled as she flipped the pancake over. "This is a small town, Graham—you can't expect to keep something like that a secret. They wrote an article about it, for goodness sake."

"She won't read the paper, Ma. I don't want her to know—promise me you won't say anything. And that Dad won't say anything if she's here when he comes back."

"What if Joyce does? Or Sheila? Or Dr. Lambert?"

I shook my head. "Don't worry about them. Please promise me."

"Whatever for?" She snapped around to me, and I lowered my forehead against the table. I didn't want to explain all this right now. "Graham, you've got to give me more than that. Tell me why you're lying—and why you want me to lie—to the girl who used to be a permanent fixture in this house and is now sleeping in the guest room after disappearing for almost a year without a single peep. You're keeping something from me."

"It's complicated."

Mom grew quiet. "You two didn't get into some sort of trouble before she left did you? You were safe?"

"God, Mom," I said, moving from the table. "It's a

little too late now for that kind of quest—"

"Answer me, Michael Graham Tucker."

"Yes, ma'am, we were safe! This has nothing to do with that. I would rather you didn't tell her."

The door creaked open from across the hall, and we both stopped talking. Cassie appeared in the doorway, and Mom smiled as big as she could. I turned away and pretended to pour myself some orange juice, even though my glass was full. I hoped she didn't hear any of that.

"Morning, honey. Want some coffee?"

Cassie smiled back. "Morning, Mrs. Tucker. That would be great."

"I'm making breakfast," Mom said. "Get yourself cleaned up and it should be ready."

"Thank you," Cassie said. I didn't turn around until I heard the door click into place.

Mom leaned against the counter so I could see her face. "So complicated that you don't even want to look at her?"

I nodded. "Promise me."

"Fine," she said. She stepped back to the stove, but I knew this conversation was far from over. "At least take a couple pancakes with you before you go."

I kissed her cheek and bolted out the door before she could change her mind.

10.

Cassie

I'D ALWAYS HOPED I would never have to re-enter the doors of St. Joseph's Memorial Hospital. It was a silly thing to dream, because there I was. Again. None of it had changed. Not the paint or the noise or the smell that really had no smell at all.

Evidence that life moved on // was everywhere but here // written in the stars // on your face // in my heart

"There's our girl," Sheila said as she wrapped me into a hug and pulled me from my thoughts. "Graham said yesterday you would be here."

"Graham was here?"

"He came every day." Every day? She pushed me away and studied me up and down. "Look at you! College must be good for you!"

I smiled. "Sometimes. Can you let Dr. Lambert know I'm here?"

"Can do. You want to see your mom? She's okay today, but I think you'll be a good fix."

I nodded, but no. I didn't want to see my mom. What

would I say after eleven months? "Sorry I abandoned you but I couldn't handle it anymore. I'm like the man who swore to love you and then left you. Left us."

⚬

MOM RESTED IN the poor excuse for the rec room in this old floral armchair. I froze at the end of the hallway, trying to find the nerve to move toward her. She looked fragile and pale under the harsh lighting. Her hair was long again, a dusty shade of dark brown, instead of the purple streaks she had the last time I saw her. She dyed it on one of her bad days—the same day that Graham proposed to me. I went to talk to her and dye was all over her clothes; she must have spilled it before she broke down on the floor. That day was bad. I had to pretend that I wasn't Cassie. I was someone else, and I'd told her Cassie was asleep, so she didn't freak out; I had to listen when she cried for me to bring my father back to her, to help her keep him.

Mom turned, and I watched as her face changed from boredom to happiness as she saw me. The smile spread across her face, bringing out the lines around her eyes. Mom was out of her chair before I could blink. She flung herself into my arms and squeezed. Even in the staleness of the hospital, I could smell the faint scent of honey soap, and with her arms wrapped around me, I was like a kid again with a mom who wasn't sick. A kid who scraped her knee or got a bee-sting and had a mom to cling to. Before I became the one she clung to instead. I almost didn't want her to let go.

"Cassidee," she whispered in my ear. "You're really

here? I'm not dreaming."

I swallowed. "Not a dream."

She ran her hand across my face. "Your hair is short, and dark."

"You like it?"

Mom dragged me toward a seat on the other side of the room, telling some of the other patients that I was her daughter, and lowered us both down onto a couch. "I love it! I think this is the style you've been missing all your life," she said. She seemed happy to see me. This was more than the meds and more than a pretty day and more than being gone for so long. This was genuine. She started rambling about how she should do her hair the same way, and I grabbed her arm.

"You're okay now?"

She waved me off. "Of course I am. You didn't have to leave school for me. You should be there. I'm sure you have a lot of classes."

I shook my head. "It's fine. I'm almost done. I'll finish everything from home. I'm here now."

Mom nodded. "Good. Can we go home? I'm ready for some real food."

"I have to meet Dr. Lambert. It's up to her when you can go."

Mom squeezed my hand, and I patted the top of hers with my other one. Mom nearly burned the house down and now she acted like I held the key to all her happiness. Once again her life was wrapped up in mine, and I wondered what else me leaving did to her. I wondered what it'd done to Graham.

DR. LAMBERT FOCUSED her stern gaze on me. "You're sure that you are up for this?"

I nodded. "I've been dealing with her bipolar disorder all my life."

"I'm aware. I'm also aware of our last conversation nearly a year ago," she said, looking at me over a pair of glasses. The last time I was in her office I'd been worried that I was bipolar. I'd felt like I'd been slipping, like I'd lost some of my own sensibility. She said it was anxiety. She'd said that sometimes, when people are dealing with someone who's sick, they feel like they have those same qualities, and that I should do something for myself. I said I had to stay—for Mom and for Graham—and she helped me see I was wrong. Then he proposed, and Mom had an episode, and I left.

"You left school to be here?" she asked.

I shifted in the chair. It was strange talking to her behind a desk. "I only have finals. They arranged for me to do them remotely. I can help out here and then go back to school or whatever I need to do."

She didn't seem to believe me. I didn't even know if I believed me. I didn't even know what I needed to do or wanted to do.

"What are you pursuing in school?" Dr. Lambert asked.

I didn't have an answer. Something, nothing, no idea. I didn't want to get into all of that with Dr. Lambert. I wanted to get Mom and go. "I'm undeclared. When can we go?"

"Come back tomorrow, and I'll draw up the papers. Graham will need to come in, since he admitted her. We'll call him," she said. I nodded. "She has to be here twice a week for a session with me. She has to take her meds. If she doesn't commit to helping herself, then we'll have to re-evaluate."

"Thanks," I said. I couldn't get out of there fast enough.

11.

Graham

I LOGGED INTO my account at Rice University's website. Any day now I could be taken off the wait-list for the undergrad program for architecture. After two years of general education courses at home, it was time to move on, and Rice was my number one. If I got in. I applied to five of the country's top ten schools, and so far, I'd only received a response from two. I was accepted into Iowa State, but not to the University of Texas. I scrolled down the site on my phone—no news yet.

"Your shake," Molly said as she handed me a protein shake and took a seat next to me. She reached a hand over the table to rest on mine, a smile on her face. She pushed a piece of blonde hair behind her ear and in a flash it wasn't her I was staring at. It was Cass.

Cass before she left, when her hair was long and her face was still bright and hopeful. We sat here, like this, me with an orange juice and her with a cup of tea. She held my hand over the table, and the ring I had just given her sparkled under the sun.

"We should tell your mom," I'd said.

She'd nodded. "I'd like to do it by myself. If that's okay? Tell her and then your parents."

And I said yes because I didn't know she would leave me to go there and never come back.

"You okay?" Molly asked. Her nose got this crinkled spot at the top of it when she was worried, and it was there now. "Is it your neighbor who's in the hospital?"

I shook my head. "My neighbor" was all I'd told Molly that Mrs. H was. I don't know if she knew Mrs. H was Cassie's mom—she knew about Cassie, but I'd never connected the dots or filled in the pieces. I didn't know how. The truth of everything was too complicated. "I was checking in on Rice. Nothing yet."

Molly leaned up on the table on her elbows. Her face was happy, and there was something about this girl that was so completely free and motivated. I hadn't met anyone like her in a long time. Cassie was like that once. "You'll get in, and you'll take the world by storm with your buildings."

"If I don't?"

Molly shrugged. "There's always Iowa State. You've been talking about this since I met you, and I think when people want something bad enough, they make it happen."

"That's a good way to view life."

"It's too short to do it any other way," she said. Something sad flashed across her face, but it was gone. I knew she had something in her past that haunted her, but she never brought it up. Molly moved toward me. She was so pretty, generous and positive. I was lucky to have her. She was solid. I needed solid.

Molly lowered herself into my lap, one leg on each side of me, and wrapped her hands around my neck. Her fingers trailed at the ends of my hair. I wondered if this was a weird place to make out. Right outside

The Good Drip seemed a little out there. But then, she smiled and I kissed her and it didn't matter anymore.

∾

MOLLY HELD MY hand as we walked from the car toward the doors of St. Joseph's. I didn't want her to come, not really, but I couldn't tell her that. She was being supportive, and even though I was only coming to sign a paper, it was good that she wanted to be here. That she seemed to care about me and what I needed.

"You've really been to sixteen countries?" I asked Molly as the hospital doors opened. I'd never left the country. We moved here as a kid and I was content to stay, mostly because Cass was here.

She nodded. "I started junior year of high school. The Model UN Club took a trip to Paris. I'd never been out of Atlanta before and I loved it."

"Model UN, huh?"

She laughed. "I went to South Africa that summer with an organization that let teens travel to help the underprivileged. Senior year I went to China, and saved all my money to backpack across Europe after graduation. Twelve weeks in Europe. I go every semester during school, too—anywhere I can. My sister loved to travel, so I wanted to go to her favorite places, and it helps me build my resume for Doctors Without Borders."

Molly was amazing. I knew how passionate she was about medicine. She wanted to do Doctors Without Borders as a nurse. She had a path, too, and I knew she would make it happen. I kissed her forehead right before the elevator doors opened. Dr. Lambert's office was directly across from the elevator, and the waiting room was empty. Molly took a seat as I approached the receptionist.

"I'm here to sign a release," I said. After a few minutes of trying, the receptionist found it and escorted me in through the door to the back of the office. I glanced at Molly, who only smiled back at me, and I felt a huge weight on me when I left the room.

12.

Cassie

I CAME OUT of Dr. Lambert's office and the receptionist wasn't sitting at her desk. The only person in the office was a pretty blonde girl on the other side of the room. I waited at the counter and looked at the clock. I wanted to get Mom and get out of there.

"She should be back soon," the girl said. She had a sweet, Southern accent. It'd been a while since I'd heard one that silky.

I nodded. "Thanks."

"I love your hair," she said.

I smiled at her. Today was the June specialty. After I chopped it off, June showed me how to put gel in it to make the back stick out like a porcupine. The front laid straight down my cheek where it was longer, and it took forever to do, but it always looked good. I lowered myself into a seat across from the girl. We waited in awkward silence for a few minutes. The only noise around us a ringing phone, the hum of the air conditioner and a ticking clock.

"Do you live here? I've never seen you before," she

asked.

I shrugged. "I used to. I'm visiting now. You?"

"I go to Francis Marion."

"Why are you in Lumberton? There's nothing here."

She smiled. "My aunt lives here so I visit a lot. The rest of my family's in Georgia, so she's the closest person. My boyfriend is here, too..."

The girl trailed off, like that last sentence explained everything. I still didn't get why someone would choose to spend time here. I'd never liked this boring town that much. That was the first thing I'd told Graham when he moved in, that this place was full of old, boring people.

"Where are you visiting from?" she asked.

"I go to Butler University in Indianapolis."

"Wow. That's quite a change," she said. "Do you like it?"

I studied the space above her. "I love it," I said. But the words didn't feel real. I wanted to love it, I thought I would, but really, it was nothing that I wanted. What I wanted was here, but even that I wasn't sure about anymore. I think I'd hurt Graham more than I could've imagined. Some things that were broken couldn't be fixed.

The receptionist appeared back at her desk, and when the side door opened, Graham appeared. My breath hitched, and words crept their way up through my throat. His eyes steadied in on me and he seemed surprised, and then his gaze drifted toward the girl across the room—who stood up—and back at me. He didn't move, but she did. Toward him.

"Ready?" she asked him.

Graham was the boyfriend. I'd been talking to his girlfriend. His very nice, Southern belle, model-like girlfriend. I was going to be sick.

He nodded. "Yeah." His back was tense, and he stuffed a hand into his pocket. I wondered if she knew that meant he was uncomfortable. He would never show it, or admit it, but there were things Graham did that didn't need to be said. That was one of them.

The girl smiled at me. "Nice to meet you. Hope you have a good visit."

Graham stole a glance at me again when she said "visit." I knew that look was me crushing his dreams again.

"Thanks," I said. Then they were gone.

Graham had a girlfriend. A girl who probably wouldn't leave him like I did or ruin him like I could. I pushed my fingers into the granite counter at the receptionist's counter. He said he wouldn't wait for me, but I guess deep down I never believed it. I pushed him away. I did this to us, and now he was with someone else. He'd done exactly what he'd promised, and exactly what I'd told him to do. He'd moved on.

ᴄᴏᴏ

I COULDN'T BRING Mom home until the next morning. She had a final therapy session and checkout procedures. Dr. Lambert was insistent that Mom understood and owned the importance of her meds and therapy—and I had a wall to fix.

Henderson's Hardware was the only local hardware shop, and I wandered through the aisles, trying to figure out what the hell I needed. I didn't know how to fix a wall. The insurance company wouldn't cover it, so I needed to do this cheap.

James Henderson appeared beside me. "How can I

help you miss—" James paused and his eyes widened with recognition. "Cassie Harlen?"

"It's me," I said.

"Well, I'll be damned." When I was a freshman in high school, James was fresh out of college then and came home to help out with the family store and to coach the girl's track team. It was only for a season, because he supposedly hooked up with a senior. I guess, like everyone else, he never left either.

He wasn't the hot stuff all the girls thought he was in high school. His belly was larger than a basketball. I crossed my arms over my chest, where he was staring intently. He was still creepy at least. "What can I do for you, Cassie?"

"I need to fix a wall."

He nodded. "I heard about the fire." There was pity in his voice when he said it.

Of course he'd heard. I was sure the whole town had. "I need to fix it. Can you do it?"

He shook his head. "Afraid I can't. I got a new construction assignment and I'll be at the Outer Banks for a month." James drummed his fingers along the shelf next to me. "Have you asked Mikey Tucker?"

"Who?" James's eyes widened. Wait... "Graham?"

He nodded. "Oh, yeah. Mikey, yea."

"Why would I ask Graham?"

"He's been helping out with us for half a year now. Boy's good with a hammer."

I shifted and zipped my hoodie nervously. Graham was Mikey now? He worked with a hammer? I didn't know anything anymore.

"Right," I said. "I'll ask Graham."

James nodded. "I'm sure he'd do it for the extra cash. He's saving up for that fancy architecture school." The bell chimed on the door, and James left me. "Excuse me."

Graham had been working construction. Architecture school. And he had a girlfriend. It seemed I didn't know him anymore.

13.

Graham

CASSIE WAS SITTING on the steps outside the garage when I got home, and as soon as I saw her, my heart started pounding. How she still made me feel like an awkward lovesick kid I'd never know. She stood when I approached, and I had no idea what she was doing outside my house. I tossed the keys in my hand, and tried to appear calmer than I felt.

"Cass," I said.

She smiled at me, and crossed her arms around her chest, and I noticed that it was a little low cut. *Don't look at her chest. Look at her eyes.*

"Mom's coming home in the morning. Thanks for going to sign that paper."

"Good," I said. "No problem."

Her eyes were so blue, and I'd forgotten how there were these little flecks of green in them. *No, eyes are bad. Look above her head. Anywhere else.*

Cassie cleared her throat. "Your girlfriend seems nice."

"She is," I said. I didn't want to talk about Molly

with her. Why was she here? *Say something to make her go away.* "Did you need something?"

She nodded. "I went by the hardware store today."

"You saw James?"

"Yeah, he got fat. And bald."

I laughed, said, "He did," and shoved my hands into my pockets. I saw her eyes focus on my hands tucked away in my pockets, and she stiffened.

"I need to get the wall fixed, and James couldn't do it."

Fuck.

"He said you'd been working with him and that I should ask you." She studied me, like she was trying to figure me out. As if I was a puzzle with no solution, even though that was really her. "He said you applied to school?"

"Rice University in Texas," I said.

She looked beyond me for a moment, then back at my face. "I know it's weird if I ask you, and you don't owe me anything."

"I'll do it," I said.

"Really?"

I nodded. Apparently I was into self-mutilation and torture. That's why I was saying yes to this. "Sure."

"Thanks," she said. She threw her arms around me, and the motion surprised me. I wasn't sure what to do, but I didn't pull away. I tried not to inhale her, but I had to know if she smelled the same. She did. I stayed in her hug, trying not feel anything I was feeling. Tried not to wonder about her, if she was happy, if she'd tell me why she left, if I'd ever stop wanting her. Because I wanted her.

I pulled away, and Cass and I stood in an awkward silence. What the hell was wrong with us? We could be adults and have a conversation. I started to speak, but there was nothing. I had no words for her, and the more I stared at her, the more I thought about how it used to be. It made me a little angry, because what used to be was all a lie.

"Really, thanks. I know I don't deserve this," she said.

"It's for Mrs. H," I said. Cass nodded slightly. In the past, she would have said something snarky to me. She would have at least smacked me for saying something like that, but she wasn't the same girl. She used to be full of life and energy; what happened to her? She changed when I proposed, and not in a good way. But now, this girl, she seemed even more lost than that one. "I'll come over in the morning and start. It should take a week."

"Great," she said.

I nodded and went past her toward my door. *Go inside, Tucker.* Being around her with all these things I haven't said was too hard. And now I would see her every day. I'm a smart one. The key clicked in the door and Cassie said my name. From the doorway, she stood in the middle of the space between our yards where half the fence laid in pieces, and pointed.

"What happened to the fence?"

I'd smashed the fence. Each time I was outside, I saw her there on that fence. Just like the day I'd met her when she was nine with a braid in her hair, red cowboy boots, asking why I'd moved here. That was where I'd kissed her for the first time, years later, mid-fight about her date with Jonas McCoy. She'd told me to stay on my side because I was immature, and I'd told her she was exhausting.

"My life isn't yours to command, Michael!" she'd yelled.

"Oh, I'm Michael now, huh?"

"When you're being an asshole—yes!"

And I'd kissed her. I'd hadn't been thinking about, it wasn't pre-planned—I'd just wanted her. After suffering through her date with Jonas McCoy, I couldn't handle her being with someone else. She was annoying as hell, and always thought she was right, but Cassie Harlen had claimed me in that spot six years before. I'd been hers ever since and she'd been mine, and I wasn't willing to lose her to Jonas McCoy.

When she left, I had to tear it down. I couldn't sleep that week after I'd gone to Indiana. I hadn't really slept well since. I kept seeing her face as she'd slid the ring back into my pocket. She was gone, but she'd still been all over Lumberton. Everyone knew her, knew us. Everything reminded me of her. The whole town was Cassie. Everyone asked me where she was, why I wasn't with her, and I had to lie over and over. That fence was the only thing I could destroy. Piece by piece, because it had to feel my pain. I'd taken an axe to it in the middle of the night, and I'd chopped until one piece of it tumbled to the ground.

Every night for a week it was all I'd done.

Then one morning I'd woken up and half the fence was in shambles, and it didn't hurt anymore.

"Big storm," I said. She crossed her arms again, but I didn't stay to let her ask any other questions.

14.

Cassie

MOM HUGGED ME again before we went inside the house and I patted her back. All this affection was different for us. Words weaved together in my head: *Too many things // I can't think to say // can't help but feel // can't understand // like why and how and if // and when // all of this will start to mend*

"Is that Graham?" Mom asked, pushing past me. The sound of the saw echoed through the house. I took a deep breath, and walked inside.

Graham had on this white sleeveless undershirt and it lay across all the new muscles on his body. I stopped to watch him, because I had to. Even though it hurt. I needed the pain to remind myself that I let him go. Everything inside me wanted to touch him again, to apologize about what happened eleven months ago. To explain. But I didn't want to ruin what he'd built. This was what I'd wanted for him all along—a life without my baggage. Now he had it, and he was better off. I'd made a mistake by hugging him yesterday—I wasn't thinking—but it wouldn't happen again.

"Hey," Graham said over his shoulder. His eyes peered into me and I froze. How could he do that with only a look? Mom turned on the record player and blared some Elton John through the house. Graham and I both looked back toward the foyer, and Mom stood in the doorway with a smile.

"I'm so glad you're here, Cassie," she said. Then, she disappeared up the stairs leaving me standing with Graham. I couldn't believe how unsure I was in front of this Graham. He was a new Graham, just like I was a new Cassie. He was stronger and surer of himself. He had a plan and dreams. The Graham I knew never had plans that didn't include me, that didn't have a future with us. *Which was why you let him go.*

Graham looked up at me suddenly, as if he'd felt me looking. We held each other's gaze across the room, and I was afraid to breathe in case he broke our gazes. He didn't until my phone rang.

"You haven't disappeared," June said when I answered.

"Not yet. I'm still intact. Mostly."

I glanced back at Graham, who was busy at work now, and walked upstairs as June rambled on. It was better if I wasn't near him.

"That's good. Three days in and it would be sucky to know you'd already dissolved." She exhaled. Probably smoking. "You aren't missing shit here by the way. I wish I could skip finals like you."

"I still have to take them," I said.

June said hi to someone she passed on the sidewalk, and I sat on my bed, tracing the outline of the circles on my comforter.

"I ran into Rohan yesterday. The band will be on tour all summer, and I guess a label made an offer."

Rohan's life improved when I left too. "It's been

three days."

"They really loved them."

"Wow," I said, playing with the embroidery on my bedspread. "Good for him."

"Has he called you?" she asked, her voice low.

"No," I lied. I hadn't answered any of Rohan's calls either. He'd left a lot of messages; his last one made it clear that we were over, and that I shouldn't call.

"I'm glad you're alive. No disappearing, Harlen."

"Promise," I said. But I wasn't sure I could keep that. Talking to June reminded me of what I wasted. Again.

"I have to go to biology. I can't wait for fucking summer." Then she hung up, and I was left standing around in my room, the sound of a saw humming between notes of "Tiny Dancer."

❦

"TIME FOR YOUR meds," I said to Mom as I put lunch in the oven. Graham was still in the living room working on the wall. Mom groaned.

"I hate this stuff," she said.

"You tried to burn the house down," I said.

"I didn't do that on purpose! Why does everyone keep saying that?" she yelled, and Graham stopped hammering. I didn't want us to put on a show for him. Or for him to worry. This wasn't his problem.

"It's what happened; whatever your intentions. You have to take your meds, you know that."

Mom reached out and stroked my hair. "Remember when you were little, Cassie? We used to drive to the beach and spend the whole day there, you and me. Remember?"

I clenched my jaw. "I remember."

"We should do it again. Let's go the beach, Cassie."

I shook my head. "Mom, take your medicine."

She ignored me, and looked past me into the distance. I could still see it all, and I knew she could too. "There was a little shop we used to go to and we'd have ice cream. I bet it's still there—"

"Mom—" I started to walk away, because I could feel a bunch of stuff flashing through my head. All the moments I clung to from the pretty days, and all the ones I didn't want to remember on the ugly ones.

Mom held on to my hand and kept me in place. "We should go again, Cassie, have one of those great days."

I snapped. "You know what I remember about those days? I remember we'd come home and I'd wake up in the morning because you were bawling or too depressed to get out of bed. And I remember missing school for days because I had to take care of you." Mom didn't move, but I couldn't stop all the wounds from bleeding out now that I'd opened them.

I was six when she'd lost me at the circus; eight at my school play she didn't come to; twelve at the movies where she forgot me; fifteen when I found her in the middle of the night in the bathtub, nearly drowning in her own bloody water and I called Graham at three in the morning, barely able to form words. He'd held me while his dad drove us to the hospital, and sat with me while we waited to see if she would live or die. He waited all through the night, and into the next morning, and missed school to be with me when we found out my mom was bipolar. He'd never let go of my hand.

"And all the times I didn't know if you were going to live. That's what I remember about those days." Mom looked horrified and dropped my hand. I pushed the pills toward her again. "So, take your pill."

There were no sounds from the living room. Which meant he was listening. He knew a lot of this, he was here for it, but we'd never really talked about it. I'd never wanted to. Mom took the pill and kissed my cheek, and when she walked away, I glanced at Graham. He leaned against the beam he'd fixed and looked in my direction. He seemed sad, and I wondered if he remembered it, too. I would've never made it through those times without him.

15.

Graham

THREE DAYS LATER and the wall had new support beams. All that was left was insulation, dry wall, and paint. Maybe two days of work and then I wouldn't have to be in this house with them all day. It wasn't bad, but I was living a fantasy, and I knew it was only a matter of time before all the walls came crashing down again. Walls that I didn't want to have to fix.

I hadn't really spoken to Cass much. I came in, did my work, and left. She had never told me about all the episodes with her mom. I remembered things, too. Sometimes she wouldn't show up for class, and when I'd get home from school, I'd watch her house from my window to make sure lights were on. The car would be gone, and they'd come home in the middle of the night or the next day. She never talked to me about any of it, but I'd known things were happening with her mom. She hadn't wanted me to tell, and I didn't want to disappoint her. Or lose her.

My phone dinged. A text from Molly about dinner tonight. I responded and glanced back up when Joyce squealed. "I love this song!" she yelled as she turned up Dean Martin.

Cass smiled too from her place in the kitchen, and they both started singing along. I was intruding. Then Mrs. H called my name and said, "You do the chorus."

"I'm working," I said, but the smile was on my face anyway. Cass smiled, too. Probably the first real smile that I'd seen in days. I'd missed her smile, that smile, the one that lit up a room.

"Come on, Graham Cracker—you know this one! I know you do," Mrs. H said.

They were both quiet as the notes before the chorus grew stronger. "Get ready!" Mrs. H yelled.

I shook my head, but what the hell? I sang the chorus as loud as I could, like we used to do when life with them was normal for me. Joyce clapped when I started, and by the end we were all singing it as if nothing had changed. And maybe it was wrong of me, but I pretended along with them.

The music swept us away and I danced around the room with Joyce. I didn't think, just moved, and Joyce passed me off to Cass. Somewhere in the laughter and the dancing and the beat, the song changed. No more swing, and instead the soft swoon of Sinatra.

Cass didn't try to leave my arms, and her being there was so right, so perfect, that I didn't make her. I stayed. She stayed, and she was pressed against my chest so that I could feel her heart beating next to mine. Her breath was on my neck as she hummed the song close to my ear. It sent shivers down my spine, and I should've stopped it, but I didn't. I couldn't. I knew what would happen when Cass got comfortable: she'd let her guard down.

There was nothing I wanted more than that, especially while she was in my arms. I wanted her there. I wanted to hold her close while she sang in my ear, because that was where she belonged. With me. In my arms. Mouth next to my neck. Music flowing from her lips right into my ear.

Her hum changed into a soft singing, so low that it could have been missed had I not been waiting. It'd been a long time since I'd heard her sing, since I had her close, and it was wrong and selfish, but I didn't want to let go. I wanted to listen.

I'd always thought Cass singing was something too personal for even me. She was like that. She found something that she loved, something that she was too afraid to lose, then she took it and held it close. Once we found a snail with a blue shell in the woods, and she thought it was beautiful so she took it home and put it in a Mason jar. It was something so precious to her that she didn't know how to share it. Sort of like I'd used to think I was to her. Always how she'd been to me.

Cass was afraid to lose things, and that fear kept her from sharing them; but eventually without room to breathe and space to move, she killed them. Just like that snail in the jar. Just like us.

Cassie's lips barely grazed my neck, and I pulled away before the song was over. She seemed as surprised as I was. I don't know if she meant anything by it, but I felt everything with that barely there touch. Things I wasn't supposed to feel. Those feelings lead to me being hurt. I couldn't be selfish this time. That never ended well with us. Not for me.

"I should get back to it," I said.

Cass nodded, and went back into the kitchen. I couldn't read her face, but that was probably for the best. I started working on the wall again, more determined to separate myself from the Harlen women than I was before. I stole one last glance at her and realized I still didn't know if Cassie was the snail or the jar, but I did know I couldn't stay around to find out.

16.

Cassie

GRAHAM STAYED ON his side of the room and barely even looked in my direction after the dance. It was so awkward now. More than before. I shouldn't have danced with him, but the song changed to Sinatra, and I'd thought to myself, *I should step away.* I'd hummed the words, because "You Go To My Head" was exactly how I'd felt. I don't even know what possessed my lips to get that close to his skin.

Graham had a girlfriend; I had no right to want to dance with him anymore, or be that close to him. But it was so normal to be in his arms again that I didn't want to end it. I didn't want there to be distance between us. I'd rested my head on his chest without thinking, and we'd moved with ease. I stole a glance up at his face, and he'd seemed to be lost in thought, and it just happened.

God. I was an idiot. I didn't know what to say.

I looked up at him from the kitchen. Music and lyrics rushed through my head, and I wrote them down as quickly as I could in my notebook.

It's crazy the way you go to my head // after all this time of words unsaid // I want to tell you the reason why // I had to leave, I had to lie // I hope we can repair the part // of me that exists in your heart // because I still can't figure out // how to move on from all this doubt // not of you but of me // and the reason we can never be

If only it was that easy. How could I tell him any of this without it making me selfish? Yes, I still loved him, but he had definitely made changes in his life. It made me wonder if I had been holding him back somehow. Was he happy now? Happier than he was with me? All I did was bring drama into his life with my problems. He had to be better now without my burdens. I didn't even deserve to be his friend. Could I be his friend after everything?

"I'm going to go now," Graham said from across the room. I looked at him from my notebook, and watched as he closed up his toolbox. "I'll be back tomorrow."

Just say it, Cassie.

Just say something. Apologize. Do something. Make it count.

"Thanks," I said. Graham nodded and then he left. So much for making it count.

If I wanted to be in his life, I had to start somewhere else. I read over the lyrics I'd written, I knew it had to be at the beginning. That was all I had wanted—to make it right—and even though being around made me want something more, I wouldn't be able to have that.

17.

Graham

THE NEXT MORNING, Bobby met me outside by my truck. I didn't really like Bobby, but he was the only one who would work for free since he owed me a favor after ditching three projects. Honestly, I was surprised he showed up at all.

"What are we doing?" he asked.

"Fixing a wall. Easy repair. A day, maybe two."

He nodded and spit some of his chewing tobacco on the ground. He walked with me to Cass's house. Joyce let us in, all smiles and nods when I introduced Bobby. Cass wasn't as enthusiastic. Bobby had been a year ahead of me in school, and two ahead of her, and when he saw Cass, he acted like he was her best friend.

"Cassie Harlen!" Bobby said, wrapping his arms around her. She squirmed, and tried to pull away, but he didn't take the hint.

"Bobby Littrell," she said weakly. He held on, and with every second, I felt myself getting annoyed. I shouldn't have felt like that, but I did.

He finally let go of her.

Cass plastered on a smile, but I knew it was fake.

Through her teeth she said, "Graham didn't mention you were coming."

"Two person job," I said. She sent me her annoyed look. At least she hadn't changed so much that I couldn't read her facial expressions. "We'll be in and out," I said.

Bobby laughed. "That's what she said."

Cass forced a bigger smile, and turned on her heel away from us. I wanted to get this job done and get out of here. Bobby was merely here to run interference. I knew if he was here, Cass wouldn't come near me. I wanted her near me, so the barrier was needed.

"Are you still seeing her?" Bobby asked.

"What?"

"You know, is she available for…" He made a circle with one hand, and pushed the other finger through it. I wanted to punch him. He stared at me. Was he seriously waiting for an answer?

"She's not available," I snapped.

"Oh, so you two are…?" he asked. I stared at him. "What happened to your other one?"

"I'm not."

"So she is?"

"No," I snapped. Bobby looked like he was going to say something else so I said, "She's not into guys anymore."

Bobby smiled. "Hot."

I really wanted to punch him.

18.

Graham

I RE-ROUTED MY morning run to go away from the Harlen house. Avoidance seemed the best way to go, and almost a month in I still didn't know what to say to Cass, or what not to say, or why I even wanted to be in her life. It was easier to not be. Then I could leave this town the next chance I got and Cass wouldn't miss me. It was a good plan. It was already the middle of May; I could make it another few months.

I rounded the corner near my place and Cassie was outside my door.

Or not.

My stomach jumped at the sight of her. How could she prance over here in that little blue sundress like it was nothing?

It is nothing. And that dress was just a piece of fabric that made her legs look really long.

Every time I saw her it was like being punched in the fucking gut. That's why I really re-routed my run, why I didn't answer when she texted me, and why I made sure to be as out of her life as possible.

"Hey," she said.

Fuck me.

"Hey," I said back, not looking at her, but I could still see her in my peripheral vision. Her short hair tucked behind her ear, as she shifted on her feet and bit the side of her jaw. That little blue dress and the way it flowed off her hips and hit her thigh. She stepped in front of me so I was forced to look down at her.

"Can we be friends?" she asked.

Of all the things I imagined Cassie Harlen might say to me, that was not one of them. *Can we be friends?* What could that even be? Could we go back to friends after everything? *Hell.*

"I just mean—" she started. She crossed and uncrossed her arms. "I know things have been weird with us, but I'm here now. I'm back. And you're here and you live next door. You are important to me, Graham."

"Important?" I raised an eyebrow. I didn't know what that meant. I was important to her when I proposed, when she said yes, and when she left. I didn't want to be that important to her.

She nodded. "I know I destroyed your trust, but I would like to start over. As friends."

"Start over." I let the words roll off my tongue. Start over with Cass.

I'd hoped for that so many times before. That one day she'd wake up and come home and ask me to start over. In all my imaginary scenarios, I agreed. But now, but this, today, I didn't know what starting over would mean. I started to shake my head when she touched my arm. Did she know touching my arm felt like a thousand needles all over my body? She dropped her hand back to her side.

Cass bit the side of her jaw. At least this was weird

for her. Me too. "You were my best friend for all my life, and it would mean a lot if you would still like to be some sort of friend. I hate that you live here and I can't even come say hello. I want to hang out with you and it not be weird."

"Not be weird?" I asked. I was only repeating what she was saying, but it was trying to sink in. Cassie wanted to be my friend. She wanted to start over, as some sort of friend. For it not to be weird. It was definitely weird. It would always be weird.

"Can we try?" she asked.

I glanced off into the distance, away from her face so things could make sense.

She was right. We'd been best friends before. Way before I kissed her and long after that. We had a relationship before we were together; maybe we could have a messed up, semi-one now. That was how friendships started, so it could be natural if we started at awkward. I'd already seen her naked—a lot—and she'd already broken my heart, so I didn't need to expect anything else from her.

Plus, I had nothing she could break this time.

"I don't know," I said. Her smile deflated, and that did me in. "I mean, we can try."

17.

Cassie

VOICES DRIFTED UP to me from downstairs, and I paused to listen. It was Graham, and I bolted down the stairs as quickly as I could. He stood in the kitchen, arm outstretched on the doorframe and looking out the back door into the yard. Just having him near made me smile. It was automatic, like breathing, natural. I paused to study him there; the boy I'd always loved, the boy who knew every single part of me better than I did. I couldn't see his face, but I didn't have to in order to know every curve of it. It was in my memory, burned there like his touch and his lips and his laugh. Graham Tucker was part of me, a large part, and that would never change.

I told him two days ago that I wanted to be friends, and I did. I could accept that we were different, that I couldn't be with him, and I would be okay. But never speaking to him again wasn't something I could give up. The thought of it knotted up my stomach. I wanted to be able to be only his friend, at least partly, but Graham still had so much of me. I hoped I could move on as much as I wanted to, as much as he had.

Mom was pointing out a few spaces around the house when I cleared my throat.

"Everything okay?" I asked.

Mom waved me off. "Graham is going to fix the AC. I didn't want to wake you."

Graham looked me up and down. I was still in my pajamas—a pair of short shorts and a spaghetti-strap tank top. Graham's eyes explored every inch of me, and his gaze on me gave me goosebumps. A slight flush filled his cheeks, and I thought of before. How before there would be no lingering looks, but him pulling me into his arms and giving in to any impulse. How his lips would trace paths on my neck, and his fingers would trail over my skin.

I met Graham's gaze, and saw the familiar look of desire there. I wasn't the only one remembering. If he was remembering, did that mean he wanted us again? I shook my head. *Stop thinking about that. You're friends now.*

He cleared his throat. "I'll get started."

Then he was out the front door. I gave Mom a disapproving look. "What are you doing?"

Mom shrugged, and slid her shoes on. "He's good at fixing things. He did it all the time while you were gone."

"I'm not gone now."

"Do you know how to fix the air conditioner?" she asked.

I shook my head. Mom looked at me for a second, appraising and satisfied with herself. Then, she poured me a glass of sweet tea. "Are you coming with me today? Dr. Lambert really wants to do the family session."

Family session. Dr. Lambert thought it would be

good for both of us to speak with her. It would help me get some answers and closure; it would help Mom understand what her episodes did to me and why it was important for her to stay on her meds. The whole thing seemed like a bad idea, which was why I'd been avoiding it for three weeks now. I didn't want to talk about the past, about the mistakes. I wanted to move forward.

"Can we do it later?" I asked.

Mom sighed. "What are you going to do here all day? Stalk Graham?"

"I don't stalk," I said, grabbing my tea and sitting at the bar.

She huffed and kissed my head. "You should talk to him."

"I did. We agreed to be friends a few days ago. He even answered one of my texts." Even the word was strange. Graham and I were friends. Not best friends. Not enemies or exes. *Friends.*

"Friends?" Mom asked.

I nodded. Mom didn't say anything else, but I could tell she had other thoughts. Luckily, I didn't have to ask what they were because the car honked, and she left to go to therapy.

I watched Graham from the window. This was not stalking. He met my gaze, and I didn't move. We stared at each other through the glass, and my mind drifted from Mom's words to the memory of his touch and my heart raced. I touched a finger to my lips, and Graham broke his stance outside with a weak wave. I waved back before bolting upstairs.

I can be your friend // I can lend a hand/ I can smile // nod and tell you my plans // I can listen, pretend // call you my friend // but in my heart // you'll be more // what you were before // with your lips // and your

hands // and the way we began // all fire and spark //
and every inch of my heart // it's what I want you to be
again // and none of that is like a friend

18.

Graham

I THREW A hammer at the air conditioning system. Piece of shit thing. I didn't know what was wrong with it. Everything should be working. All the wires were connected but the fan wouldn't start. This thing was probably a goner.

"Want some water?" Cass asked. I glanced up and she came toward me with a glass of water. With each step something inside me jumped in anticipation of being near her. I'd been thinking about her all morning, ever since I saw her in the hallway and she looked so beautiful there. Earlier when I watched her through the window, before she saw me, and just stared because having her here, even though she wasn't with me, was right. I hated myself for it; I wanted to see her and feel nothing.

But I did. I felt more than I wanted to admit. I was probably a goner, too.

She held out the glass, and our fingers grazed. I let my fingers linger near hers, her cool, smooth skin to my warm, rough skin. It was perfectly comfortable, like my hands were supposed to be there. *Except they aren't.*

"Thanks," I said, pulling back the glass.

Cassie nodded. "Any luck?"

I gulped the water down in one sip. "No idea."

"Thanks for checking it out," she said.

"I think I'm going to go," I said. "You should call someone else about it."

"Okay," she said, moving to sit on the steps.

I guess that was it. I gathered my tools and my flannel and took a couple steps toward my house. Something stopped me. She seemed upset about something. *Don't talk to her about this. Walk away.*

"You okay?" I asked. *So much for walking away.*

I lowered myself next to her on the step. We sat close together there, legs only less than an inch from touching. I knew it was as close as I could get before I lost control of my senses. Cass stretched one arm out over her leg so her fingers dangled at her knee. Her fingertips brushed my leg, and it was only a second, but it sent shocks through my body. My fingers twitched to reach out for hers, to connect our bodies in some simple way so she was part of me again. Being around her was a drug, and I wanted to have some. Any closer and I'd be in trouble.

"It's hard being here, you know?"

Shit, I knew. It was always hard being here, especially after all this. She was different now, and I still didn't know why. I didn't know what I'd done to her to make her leave like that. I wanted to ask, but I didn't think I'd like the answer. If we were moving on, there was no reason to drudge it up.

"I thought I had it together, and now I'm back and I feel like I don't know where I'm going next. What happens tomorrow?"

I scoffed. We'd had this conversation a hundred times in our life. Cassie was never sure of where she wanted to be; as long as it wasn't Lumberton, North Carolina, she would be happy. I lowered myself to the spot beside her.

"You can't live your life in fear of what could be or you'll never live it."

Cass looked at me, her blue eyes piercing into mine. "That's the Graham I know."

"I'm still the same." *You're the one who's changed.*

"No, you're not, *Mikey.*"

She laughed and bumped my shoulder. My whole body responded to the touch, and it seemed like every cell of me was a frayed nerve ending that Cass could make react. I gritted my teeth to hold myself back from her. How could her being gone make her touch more electric than before?

"They call me that at work. That's all. You, Mrs. H and Mom are one of the few people who called me 'Graham,'" I said tightly. I was trying to keep my composure here and she wasn't making any of it easy. Not with her touches and her smile and her being Cass.

Cass laughed, and the sound was sort of awesome. So warm and light. I missed that, too.

"Why are you working with James, anyway?"

I shrugged. "I needed money and people around town needed help. I fell into it, but the pay is good and when I'm at Rice I'll be a little better off."

"You're really going?" she asked.

"I'm on the wait list, but I'm holding out. Should be any day now."

Cass looked at me, really looked at me, and I wondered what she was thinking. Did she think this was a crazy plan? Did she wish I wasn't going? Did she really care about it at all?

"You'll get in," she said, brushing away a piece of her loose hair. I used to be the one who did that. "I have no doubt."

I smiled softly. Whatever she'd been through, she was still so sure of me. She'd told me she hadn't been so sure of herself, of what she wanted, for a long time, but you'd never know it from looking at her. She'd carried herself with so much confidence. At least I'd thought. "What about you? What's next?"

She took off her flip-flop, slid it back on. "I don't know yet." Silence spread between us, but it was brief. "I was thinking about Texas, but it's pretty hot there. I heard that was why they all liked to wear hats."

I laughed. She was thinking about Texas. She didn't mean that, so I let it go. "I'm pretty sure that's not true."

Cass pushed me gently, bringing back those rumbles in my body. If this was my new reaction to her then I wanted her to touch me again and never stop. "Then, why do you think they all wear those cowboy hats? You should get one of those cowboy hats."

"I'm not getting a cowboy hat," I said with a smile. This was Cassie—a glimpse of her, anyway. The one who was laughing next to me and joking, almost like we used to.

"You'd look good in a cowboy hat," she said, staring again.

I met her gaze, and in her eyes I saw more than I could explain. A past that was so entwined there was no distinction between her and me. The future that I'd wanted for us where we were together and we had everything we wanted because the most important thing was each other. And I saw the present, the right now, where we were strangers sitting on a porch. Strangers who could never really be strangers because we knew each other in and out. I reached out and pushed that piece of hair behind her ear. I had to touch her, to remind myself that the past was over and the present was some messed up reality where we'd never get that future I wanted. But maybe I could be okay with another future where Cassie and Graham are completely just friends.

I pulled my hand away and leaned back against the step. "Tomorrow, we should go do something fun."

"Something fun?"

I nodded. "Yeah. Go somewhere. Friends can go places, right?"

I hoped the answer was yes, because otherwise, I shouldn't have asked that question. This was fire. Friend or not. What was I doing?

"Yes," she said. She smiled, and her whole face was practically glowing. I loved that I was the one to put that smile there. Even as an awkward some kind of friend. I could do this. I was hanging out with a friend. A friend who made me feel like I could walk through fire or scale buildings and walk away without a scratch. A friend I'd sacrifice anything for, as crazy as it was to do that.

"Graham?" Molly called. I jumped up from the stair and started to walk toward her, but she was already on her way over. She'd already spotted Cassie next me. "What are you doing?" she asked.

"I was helping out with some things around here," I said, moving closer to Molly. I hadn't told her that the girl in the hospital was Cass. I had to get out of there. "I'm done for now though."

"I've seen you before," Molly said. She focused past me on Cassie. "At the hospital. I'm Molly." She held out her hand.

Cass shook her head and reached for Molly's hand. "Right, you're the girlfriend. I'm Cassie."

Molly's eyes darted toward me, and her mouth made a little O. In a flash, her focus was back on Cass. "I didn't realize the connection." Molly studied the house. I was in trouble for not telling her everything about Mrs. H and the fire and the girl next door being the girl in the hospital.

"We should go," I said, and I dragged Molly away before anything else was said.

We were going into my apartment when she said, "That was Cassie?"

"Yep."

"And her mom was the neighbor in the hospital? The one you saved from the fire?"

"She was."

"And she's back now?"

"Yep."

"How long?"

"Don't know?"

"And you're hanging out with your ex?"

"She's just my neighbor."

Molly raised her eyebrow, as if she was waiting for me to say something else. I didn't say it. I should've said other things. I should've said there's nothing between us, that she's only an old friend, a part of who I used to be, but when I was about to say it, I couldn't.

19.

Cassie

I DIDN'T THINK Graham would really carry through his plan of doing something together—as friends— but he called me first thing the next day, and within a few hours we were packed in his truck listening to The Avett Brothers. They weren't really my choice, but they weren't bad. There was this sound to them that reminded me of Graham. An easy-going, folksy, high-energy vibe that shouldn't go together, but it did.

The best things didn't seem to go together at first.

I reached over to turn down the air, just as he reached over to turn up the music and our elbows bumped. "Sorry," I fumbled.

"Hot?" he asked.

I nodded, and he changed the air, but I wasn't so sure it was just the outside. Graham rested one hand on the wheel and the other on the seat. I looked down at it. There was only a little bit of space between us, and usually I'd sit in the space so there was nothing, and he'd drive with one hand on the wheel and the other on my thigh. But I couldn't sit there now, so I sat with the few feet between us where his hand rested on the seat, outstretched, and in my head he was waiting for me take it.

When the song ended, he moved his hand and tapped his fingers on the steering wheel as he drove, and I wondered if he liked this song or if he was nervous. Maybe he was both. I know I was.

I'd tried not to think about it while I was getting dressed. Not to worry about being cute or how my hair was or debate mascara, because mascara could mean something more than a day with a friend. But I'd kept hearing his voice on the phone: *"Do you want to hang out today?"* He was all jittery, a way I hadn't seen him since middle school, and two hours later I still hadn't been dressed. Graham was my *friend.* We were *friends.* That was all I would get, so it had to be enough. I wanted it to be enough because I knew how lucky I was to get that chance. How lucky I was to be sitting in his truck listening to not-too-horrible music. That's why I'd put on mascara.

"So, where are we going?" I asked over the music.

Graham jumped a little, almost like he forgotten I was sitting there. I hoped that wasn't what it was. "It's actually a sur—"

"Don't you dare say, 'surprise,' Graham Tucker, or I will smack you."

He chuckled, and turned down the music. "You wouldn't dare."

"Try me. Say it."

Graham stopped at a red light. "I would never; I know you hate surprises." *Right.* Graham knew everything I liked, and everything I didn't. "I was going to say: it's actually a surpris*ing* story." He exaggerated the ending and paused for dramatic effect. I'd give him drama. I stuck my tongue out at him.

Graham shook his head and started driving. "Fine. I won't tell you."

"What's the story?" I asked.

"Nope," he said, his eyes sparkling. When he let go he was more and more like that little kid at Christmas. His eyes made him seem that way when he was really happy. It allowed me to forget that I'd walked away from us. I felt like myself, and the only reason was because of him. That was all he'd ever expected me to be. "Frankly, darling, you've lost the privilege."

I pressed a hand to my chest, and grabbed Graham's arm with the other. Touching him, even my hand on his arm, felt natural. It was where I was supposed to be. With my best Scarlett O'Hara voice—which I had perfected because our ninth grade teacher made us read the book, watch the movie and then perform scenes from it in front of the class the last week of school before summer and we hated it since it was worth like 20 percent of our final grade—I said: "Tell me, Graham Tucker, or I will just die!"

Graham was smiling when he looked back at me and I felt myself smiling. I didn't have to pretend to be someone else or hide any part of myself. He looked at me with the sparkle and some fire, and I felt like I was flying. He did that to me, made me drop all the pretenses and the masks and just be his Cass. Where was he taking me? Maybe it was a date-date place. Maybe it was a friend place, but it could be a date-date place.

"I'm taking you to Rinkydinks."

Rinkydinks? Nothing said "friends" like ugly, plastic bowling shoes. My heart sank, but I tried to keep my smile up. I leaned back against the seat. What was I expecting? We'd had a moment, but Graham made himself clear. We're friends. That was all this was supposed to be, anyway. *Get it together, Cassie.*

"Rinkydink Ted's Fun Plaza is still around?"

"No, no," he said, shaking his head. "Not Ted's anymore. It's Barb's," he said. I laughed a little. They finally divorced. Ted and Barb Dinkleman were the worst couple ever. We used to go to their bowling alley in high school because they served underage beer, let us use the gutter guards, and entertained us when Barb and Ted would have fights on the floor. They used to yell across the alleys and over the loudspeaker and once they even rolled balls at each other to see who would trip or yell or walk away first. We had this friend named Lila who used to find ways to make them start fighting.

"It's just 'Rinkydink's' now."

"Why is this a surprising story? They were destined for divorce."

"That's not the surprising part. They got divorced because Ted fell in love with George."

I gasped. "The creepy maintenance guy?"

Graham nodded. "Right? Anyway, Barb got ownership and rebuilt the whole thing. It has lasers and black lights, a decent snack bar, an arcade—" Graham paused and he had this sly side smile on his face and his eyes were wide. "—and Bobo the clown."

"A clown?" I asked. She always wanted a clown.

"No kidding," he said.

"That's crazy," I said with a smile. This town was weird. I turned so I could see Graham better and curled my legs up into the seat. His face was a little scraggly today and I liked him with some scruff. It always made him look more rugged. Not that I was thinking about that.

"What?" he asked, voice rough.

"I can't wait to kick your ass in bowling," I said

instead.

"You won't kick my ass," he said.

I shook my head. "Do you remember the Summer of the Reckoning?" That was the summer before junior year. We called it that because Lila and Adam broke up and we could only be friends with one of them at a time. "I believe I won that competition trophy."

"Maybe I let you win," he said, his eyes wide and mischievous.

I stared at him. "You didn't."

"Seriously?" He raises an eyebrow at me. "You think I really didn't see that sleeper pin in the last frame?"

"The ball wasn't even near it."

"Yeah, I know," he said with a half-cocked smile.

I slapped his arm. "You let me win?"

"You were my girlfriend."

"So?"

"I wanted to get laid," he said. I slapped his arm again. "Hey! I was sixteen. You can't blame me for that."

"I can't believe you," I said as he put the car in park.

"I knew what I wanted."

I looked at Graham and he was studying me too, his eyes burning into mine. I tried to look away, but they captured me. I didn't know what to say, and I tried to find the right words but that only made me more nervous.

My head spun as all the moments played back for me. Him kissing me for the first time near that fence. The look on my mom's face when he came over for dinner and kissed me at the door. The first time we had sex in his bedroom. The night of the bowling challenge, after I won that trophy and we spent the whole night in the room above the garage.

"We should go in," Graham said, finally breaking our gaze. I nodded and followed him out of the truck, but I was pretty sure my heart was left on the floor.

The outside was covered in some sort of metal, almost like a tin can, and there were bright circles all over the walls, like polka dots. The old place was a boring shade of brown, but this was fun. The building twisted and turned. It almost felt like Wonderland.

"This place is cool," I said, getting out of the car.

"I know," Graham said. We walked side by side into Rinkydinks, and he bumped my hip as we moved. My whole body flushed, but I knew it didn't mean anything for him. I had to get it together. My mind needed to be put on a leash.

"No letting me win," I said.

Graham opened the door for me. "We're friends now; no pretending this time for bonus points."

Right. No pretending. We were just friends now, even though I was pretty sure people who were just friends didn't have all these sparks. All of these questions and feelings and thoughts. Friends didn't have to pretend they were just that.

"No worries," I said.

Except if I didn't pretend, I'd never be able to stand near him without wanting to kiss him.

20.

Graham

BARB DINKLEMAN COOED when I walked up to the desk. Cassie waited beside me, oddly quiet. It didn't matter. Not talking was better. Bowling was a bad idea. I thought it was better than a dark movie theater, but there was too much downtime in bowling, too much talking. But in the car, it was easy. She was Cass and I was Graham and it was fine. We could do this. We could hang out.

"Mikey, honey! You're here!"

"Yes, ma'am," I said. I hoped she wouldn't make a scene, but she glanced between me and Cass, flailing her bright bracelet-covered arms, and I could tell a scene was coming. "We're here to bowl, Mrs. Dinkleman."

She waved me off. "Call me, Barb, Mikey. You know you can do that." She glanced past me to Cass. I could tell she recognized her from the scrutinizing expression on her face—or at least thought she did. I cleared my throat to get her attention.

"Barb, one lane please, ma'am," I said with a smile.

Mrs. Dinkleman chomped some gum and smiled at me. "Of course, honey." She pushed some buttons on the computer, and printed me out a ticket. I really wanted to get out of her way. "Lane Twelve. Need some shoes?"

"Size eleven," I said. I looked over my shoulder at Cassie.

"Eight please," Cass said. She stood beside me, shoulder-to-shoulder, and smiled. This was normal for friends. Completely. Mrs. Dinkleman handed us the shoes and I thanked her.

"Anything for you, Mikey," she said with a smile. Before the divorce, she never smiled. Cass's eyes bored into me as we walked to our lane. I could see the wheels turning. How long would it take her to ask me about it?

We turned into the lane, and put on our shoes. We didn't really speak to each other, and I kept thinking that this was the dumbest idea I could've had. I shouldn't have brought her here or even agreed to try this friend thing. Now what would we do?

"I'm going to get a ball," Cass said.

I nodded in her direction, lost in my thoughts, and then put our names in the computer. We did this once before, back when it was Rinkydink Ted's, and our friends always gave us couple names. Brad and Angelina. Bonnie and Clyde. Peanut Butter and Jelly. Whatever they could think of. I stared at the blinking cursor. I wanted to do that again, to be those famous couples, but we weren't. Were there famous friends? I typed her name instead, and it was wrong, so I backspaced.

Cassie poked me on the shoulder.

"Did you poke me?"

She smiled and shrugged. "What was up with Mrs.

Dinkleman?"

Five minutes. A record for sure. "I helped out around here when it was first renovated."

"You worked here?"

"Sort of."

"What'd you do?"

I took a breath. "Designed it."

Her eyes widened. "You designed this?"

I nodded. "She came to me after Mr. Mykiam—remember him? He taught art and was one of her leaders for the Wednesday night bowling league—he wrote me a letter for school and he got me involved with the designing and the building plans."

"Wow! You did all this?" She looked around the room, and I could see the pride in her face. It was not what I expected to see. Cassie's eyes were as bright as her smile. It imprinted this moment into my brain. I never thought that I'd get to share this with her, and to have her love it like this made me feel like I had a purpose. Like my dream was something we could share again. I stood next to her. It really was amazing looking at something I designed and watching other people get joy from it. Especially her.

I poked her and she laughed. "I didn't do the polka dots."

"Too bad. That's the most inventive part," she said before she turned around to put a silver bowling ball on the return. I grinned because I knew she was kidding. She always got this tone when she was kidding.

God, that girl. Crazy how she still sent me spiraling, and after all that time, I thought it would've passed. If I was sane I'd step away, put space between us but that was the last thing I wanted.

"You ready to lose, Tucker?" Cass called.

"Ready if you are," I said. I clicked the scorecard on

the computer console. "You're first."

Cass turned toward the screen. Grabbing her ball, she stepped into position. The screen flickered to life and her name popped up. She squealed. "Mr. Hyde?"

I raised an eyebrow. "And Dr. Jekyll."

"Those are horrible nicknames."

"We are a horrible man," I said. Cass shook her head. She hated that book. It was the great rampage of sophomore year.

I watched Cass as she put her feet on the little dots. One, two, three, and she let go of the ball; it rolled straight down the middle and knocked down eight pins. She smiled back at me. "It's a good start, Doctor."

I laugh. "This is only the beginning, Mr. Hyde."

21.

Cassie

GRAHAM WON. WE were in the car laughing about the night, "River" by Joni Mitchell (my pick) playing in the background around us. I had fun, and I'd forgotten how much fun Graham could be; he always knew how to make me smile. Somehow all of that got lost in my head. I didn't want the night to end, but he pulled up in the spot between our houses.

We sat in his truck, neither of us moving at first. I didn't know why he was frozen, but I knew why I was. This had been a great night, and now what? How did we go back to pretending? Or had we been pretending all night? No, we hadn't. I hadn't. That was too natural to be fake. I didn't like fake us; I liked the real thing.

I unbuckled my seatbelt. Someone should move, and even though I didn't want to, it had to be me. He'd made himself very clear, and I wondered if that had changed now. But I couldn't ask; it wasn't fair.

"I had fun," I offered.

Graham's smile faded when he looked at me. I wondered what he was thinking. He had to be thinking something. Had I upset him again somehow?

"Thank you," I said.

He cleared his throat. "Of course. Let me walk you home."

It was an old joke between us, since my home was maybe thirty feet from his. He used to come around and open my door. We'd held hands and lingered outside the truck, lingered on the sidewalk, lingered on the porch. We'd always lingered, always tried to hold on for another hour, or minute, or heartbeat.

He didn't open my door today. He waited outside the truck for me, and we walked in silence toward my house. There wasn't much room between us, and if I moved a little closer we'd be touching, but I didn't. It was torture, actually, because despite my senses my hands wanted to be in his. I didn't know where to put my hands or how to handle his silence or block out the memories.

Would walking so close to him and not touching him ever feel normal? Laughing all night and not kissing him? What was I going to do about my feelings for him? I couldn't ruin this new life of his by trying to force myself into it. I wouldn't be able to live with myself knowing I was responsible for his heartbreak again. I had to get it together.

"I'm glad we did this," he said. I looked up at him. It was painful because I could see that he meant it. And because I was glad too, even though I hated myself for wanting it. "I like being your friend. It's where we started."

Next to me // next to you // I want to be next to you // hold my hand // linger there // you and me are everywhere

I nodded. "I like it too, Graham."

We climbed the five steps to my front porch.

"Well—" I start.

"On Friday a bunch of the old gang is having dinner—Lila, Eric, McCoy—because Hannah's in town for the weekend. You should come."

In my pocket, "It Ain't Me Babe"—Johnny and June Carter Cash version—started playing. I didn't even remember turning on the ringer. It was June, that was her ringtone. I ignored it.

"They won't mind if I come?" I asked. Aside from one email from Lila, I hadn't heard from any of them since I left. That email wasn't on the best of terms— she sent it right after Graham came to school, and I rejected him. I knew I'd lost them all in the break-up, and I hadn't blamed them.

Graham shook his head. "No, it will be nice. Low key. We're going to dinner at Lou's."

"Okay," I said.

He smiled. "Friday."

"Friday," I said. With a nod, Graham crossed the yard and when he was gone, I exhaled and went inside.

MOM WAS RUNNING late the next day, so I had to park the car instead of waiting in the pick-up zone. Since I parked the car, I had to go upstairs to get her from Dr. Lambert's office so I could get my parking validated. Small town doctor offices shouldn't have validated parking.

Dr. Lambert was standing in the lobby of her office with Mom. "Cassie, so good to see you," she said.

"You, too Dr. Lambert." I held out the ticket. "Could you?"

With a smile, she took it from my hand and passed it on to her receptionist. "I've been trying to get you in for a session for a month now, Cassie. When can you come? You're still interested in me helping your mother, yes?"

I should've known this was a set up. Mom never made me wait. "Sure."

"Let's say Monday?"

I nodded, and Dr. Lambert handed me the ticket. "Great. I'll see you at ten."

I looked over at Mom, but she shrugged. "Ten it is."

On the way to the car, Mom asked me about last night. "You didn't say anything this morning."

"It was good."

"Good?"

I nodded. I didn't know what else to call it. We went. We'd had fun. We hadn't fought. It had almost been normal.

Almost normal // you and me // that's the most we'll ever be // some sort of friends // you and me // that's the way the story ends

Mom tapped the roof of the car while I dug out the keys. "Good isn't the answer I expected."

"What did you expect?"

Mom's forehead scrunched with lines. Sometimes, I forgot that she was getting older. In my head she would always be the carefree, young, enthusiastic Mom who taught me about music. I wasn't even sure anymore which pieces of that person were real and which ones were the disease. "Cassie, when you were teenagers, the two of you couldn't even be in a room together without making me feel like I was intruding. Anyone could look at you and know you were in love. That was real, too, more real than anything I've had, and you're telling me that you spent a night out with

Graham and it was just 'good'?"

I shook my head and unlocked the car door. "He has a girlfriend, Mom. What else is it supposed to be?"

"You came back here for him."

I scoffed. "I came back because you needed me." I yanked the door open. I hated that she knew the part of me that I didn't like to admit out loud.

"I know you, Cassie. You're still in love with him. Why did you even leave?"

I slammed my car door shut and turned the key. "I don't want to talk about this with you. Graham doesn't want me. Last night was fun, two long-time friends going bowling. It was hardly a date or anything romantic. He doesn't feel that way. So can we stop now? Please?"

She raised her hands in defeat and I backed out of the parking lot.

22.

Graham

"HEY BABE," I said, answering Molly's call.

"You aren't at dinner yet, are you?"

"About to walk in," I said. I scanned the parking lot at Clyde's for Cass. She was meeting me here and even though I said it was okay, I'd had two days to think about it and our friends didn't know Cass was coming. I hoped that wasn't a stupid decision.

"I'll be quick. Aunt Kat wants you to come to brunch tomorrow at noon. Can you do it?"

Cass waved at me from the car as she pulled in. My heart raced at the sight of her. This was fire, I knew that, but we could be friends. We were mature.

"I can do that," I said.

"Great," Molly said. Cass's car door closed, and she walked toward me. It seemed like nothing had changed in that moment. She was walking toward me like she'd never walked away from me. Back when we were hopeful and naïve and in love. Had that only been a year ago? It felt like yesterday and a lifetime.

"Awesome. I'll talk to you later, okay?" I said. I ended the call before she could respond. I'd probably hear about that later.

"Hey," Cass said.

She looked nice. Cass had on this jean jacket over her green dress that brought out the green in her eyes. Her hair was flat and straight, and it was getting longer, so it was easy to imagine it the way it used to be. The way I used to run my hands through it when I kissed her, or wipe it out of her face so I could see her better when she was under me.

"You okay?" she asked.

Play it cool. I shrugged. "Just hungry," I said. I opened the door and followed her in, letting my hand slide to her lower back. She glanced back at me, but didn't say anything.

Inside, Clyde's wasn't that busy yet. It didn't really get crazy until later when Lou came on the clock. I heard McCoy before I saw any of them. He had one of those voices that carried in the crowd. It was probably from all his years as football quarterback. Cass pressed in next to me, and I could tell she was nervous. I really hadn't thought this through.

McCoy saw me first, and my name echoed through the bar. "Tucker!"

I wasn't sure how he became part of our group. I didn't really like the guy—never had. Especially with the way he'd always looked at Cass back before we were together. After we started dating, McCoy hooked up with Lila. A lot. So, he always stayed around. McCoy, Hannah and I graduated, the rest of the group stayed in school. McCoy went to Georgia to play ball; Hannah went to Ithaca; I stayed here for Cass. That was all there was, really.

I shook McCoy's hand. Hannah and Eric smiled, like they were happy to see me. Lila bounced into my arms for a hug. Everyone sort of froze after that, and they all zeroed in on Cassie. Cass, who stood awkwardly behind me and bit the side of her cheek. *Say something, Tucker.*

"Harlen?" McCoy asked.

"Hey, Jonas."

Everyone was a statue, all eyes on her. Lila looked from Cass to me, and I knew what she wondered. I shook my head very slightly, and Lila turned away. Great start.

"Damn, you look good," McCoy said.

Everyone laughed after that, but my stomach never settled. The tension was broken, even if it was only for now. We all sat at the table, and I told myself this was good. Cass was here. If she could patch it up with me, then she could reconnect with her old friends. She could get whatever closure she needed, and we could all move on.

"What are you doing this summer?" Lila asked Hannah.

Hannah flipped her hair and smiled. "Puerto Rico! I leave next week. You?"

"Mom wants us to go visit Grandma so I'm sure I'll be stuck in Florida most of the summer watching old people in the retirement home try to skinny dip," Lila said.

Eric would stay at school for the second half of the summer and take more classes. And he seemed excited, but he always loved school.

I stole sideways glances at Cass while McCoy talked about his plans of football and girls. Something inside me was glowing when she met my gaze. I was fucking crazy. I knew that much, but watching her try made me feel like trying. What I was trying to do though was another question.

Hannah cleared her throat and shook her head.

Lila perked up in her seat as she said Cassie's name. "Why are you home? Are you here all summer?" she asked.

Cass bit the side of her jaw. None of them ever knew about her mom. She'd kept that secret closely guarded. "I'm here for my mom. I don't really have a plan yet beyond this."

"You mean for the summer?" Eric asked.

Cass shrugged. "I mean, in general."

"You aren't going back to school?" Lila asked.

She twirled the straw in her drink. Her eyes locked on mine. Cass was nervous, I could see it, but she was trying to keep it together. "I don't know yet. It depends."

"On what? I thought you loved school. It was the whole reason you left us all without a word and then disappeared." Cass looked at Lila and I kicked Lila under the table.

She kicked me back. "No offense or anything, but I'm confused about why you wouldn't go back to a place that you obviously adored. There's nothing for you here anymore."

Cass didn't respond, but I could see on her face that she was upset. I wished I didn't know how to read her, that I didn't know what Lila was doing—or why. Lila looked at me with her eyebrow raised.

"Have you heard back from Rice yet?" McCoy asked me. I may not have liked him, but he'd saved me from saying something to Lila I didn't mean.

"Yeah, what's going on with that? When are you escaping the clutches of this place?" Hannah asked.

The four of them reverted focus to me, and waited for a response. "I haven't heard yet, but school starts in August."

"You'll hear from them and then you'll never have to think about all the trash you left behind," Lila said, sending me the biggest smile in the world.

They changed the subject after that. Started talking about football and whether the Cowboys would beat the Panthers again. Throughout dinner Hannah kept shooting me knife eyes. She didn't approve. Not that there was anything to approve.

"Excuse me," Cassie said suddenly. She threw her napkin down on her plate and headed toward the restroom. I watched her, trying to figure out if she was okay, but she was too quick. This night was not going as planned.

Lila smacked me on the arm.

"What the hell are you doing?" she asked.

I took a drink. Everyone at the table was staring at me. "What?" I asked. But I knew what.

"How could you bring her here?" Lila asked.

"Are you screwing her again?" McCoy asked.

"What happened to Molly?" Hannah asked.

"I think he's lost his mind," Eric said.

The questions came fast, and I stared at all my friends. "It's not like that. She's just Cassie."

"Exactly! Do y'all remember what happened to Graham after Cassie chose school over him? Because I do," Lila said. "I believe it was something like drink, break a fence, not shower, wreck a car, drink some more, burn things, tear down a fence, sleep." She counted it all on her fingers.

"You forgot mope," Eric added.

"And swear hatred of her forever," Hannah added.

I crossed my arms. "Nothing's going on with us. She's here because of her mom—that's all."

"That's never all. Not with you and not with her," Lila said.

"I'm with Molly," I said. I had to convince them that nothing was happening between us. If they didn't believe me, no one would. It was nothing. *Nothing.*

"I saw how you looked at her. That's not the face of a man with another girl," McCoy said. He didn't have room to talk, anyway. He'd never kept a girl longer than a week.

"She's my friend," I said.

"But you have feelings for her," Eric said.

"No." I slumped into the booth. This rapid fire was exhausting.

"You're letting her in again. She's going to ruin everything," Lila said.

"She broke your heart," Hannah said.

Hannah said it like she was there when I woke up without Cassie. No one would ever understand that feeling. I'd thought something had happened, and I'd waited for a few hours, but I knew something was wrong. I felt it. Then her mom told me she'd left to go to school in Indiana, and my future crashed and burned.

I looked at Lila. "I know that. Trust me, I remember it."

"Are you really stupid enough to let her do that again?" Lila asked.

"She's not going to break my heart, Lila."

Lila shook her head. "You're an idiot."

"Can we change the subject?" I asked.

"Sure," Hannah said, leaning in. "Y'all remember that time when Graham went all the way to Indiana to find the girl who left him in the middle of the night, only to come back with a lame-ass story and a ring he couldn't return so he sold it for half the price on Craigslist?"

I ran a hand down my neck. I hated this. I wasn't doing anything wrong—but they were right. All of that had happened. I'd driven all the way to Butler to watch her take off my ring. It was one of those dramatic slow-mo moments in those movies. I'd used to think those were stupid, but that's how I'd seen it. That's how it felt. It was happening and I had no control over it. I couldn't pause. I couldn't skip ahead. I'd told her then that if I left I wouldn't go back there. I wouldn't wait for her. If I left, it was for good, and I'd meant it. And she gave me back the ring, so I'd left.

"I remember," Eric said. "It took him months to get it together. I'd hate to see that happen again."

McCoy cleared his throat, but Lila spoke again before he could. "How can you forgive her for that? What she did was horrible."

"Open your eyes before she does it again," Hannah said.

McCoy cleared his throat louder. We all looked up this time, and Cassie was standing at the end of the table. She'd heard us.

"I have to go," she said. How much had she heard? "It was good to see y'all."

Before anyone could respond, she grabbed her purse from the seat next to McCoy and bolted out the door. I watched her go, and my immediate thought was that I should go after her. I should make sure she was okay.

"Don't do it," Eric said. "This time, don't do it."

He meant don't go after her this time. Don't follow her.

"You don't owe her anything. Do you even know why she left?" Lila asked.

"No," I said. I drummed my fingers on the table. Everyone was in agreement and I was a dumbass. They were right. I wasn't thinking.

It was quiet for a minute, and then McCoy ordered us all another round from Lou, and this time, I stayed.

23.

Cassie

WHEN I GOT home, Mom was already asleep. Her meds made her tired, and I was grateful I didn't have to explain my evening. I didn't want to be reminded—again—of all my mistakes. Mom didn't understand it, not really. How did I explain everything without making her feel bad? It was her bipolar disorder that made me afraid, her mistakes. In being so scared of them, they became mine. I was destined to be like her, if for no other reason than I made myself like her.

I put on some pajamas and debated calling back June. She called again during dinner, but I didn't answer. To call her meant I had to tell her everything. Starting at the beginning of Graham and me would take hours, and I wasn't in the mood.

I went to a blank page in my notebook and let the pencil slide across it until more of my own notes appeared. In Indianapolis, I kept myself busy so I didn't have to think. But here there was nothing else. I tapped into that part of me and let the notes pour on to the page.

You show up at my door // The first thing you say // is I'm beautiful and you miss me // I push you away and say you shouldn't be here // it's a lie and all I want is you near // you beg me to tell you // what can you do to make me come back to you // You say you didn't even know how much I wanted to go // And if I love you all I have to do is say so...

Sometimes love is not enough // when it means losing // I can't watch you walk away // love doesn't always build a dam // sometimes it's not enough // cause love means you stay // and I can't let you hurt that way

I threw the pencil down. That is not forgetting, it's remembering. It was exactly like they'd said: Graham came to me at school and I made him leave. I did this to us, and that wasn't something I wanted to deal with either. Had it really been that bad for him? No wonder they all hated me. I hated myself for it.

Instead, I went to the record player and combed through other people's music. I had no idea what I wanted to listen to. Soft crooning? Loud metal? Jazz? The options were limitless. I scanned the collection and put on Bob Dylan. *Blood on the Tracks* seemed fitting. The record popped as it started to play, and I turned it up enough to hear it through the house, but low enough that it didn't wake Mom.

The doorbell rang, and I saw the top of Graham's head through the little window on the door. I pressed my head against the wood of the door. I didn't want to answer because I was weak and afraid of what he'd say to me, or worse, what the words would do to me. We'd come so far in the last few weeks.

Graham knocked on the door, and it echoed in my ears. I sighed before answering.

"Hey," I said. Graham stood on the porch, hands in

his pockets. His eyes were glassy, like he'd drank too much. I squeezed my fingers into a fist at my side in order to keep them from reaching out.

"Got a minute?" he asked. His voice was lower and rougher than usual.

I stepped out onto the porch. The May air was warm, but not too hot yet. He stepped back and leaned against the railing of the front porch. I bit down on my lip. We both stood there in silence. This was becoming a thing between us—silence—and I wanted to fill it. Words didn't seem to work, though. There were only so many ways to apologize and so many ways to pretend. Only so many ways to hold myself back from what I really wanted.

"I'm sorry about that," Graham said. "I didn't think it would be like that."

I shook my head. I only wanted to forget all about the night out with my old friends. Trying to forget was my theme song. "I don't blame you—or them. I knew they hated me."

"They don't hate you," he said.

I crossed my arms. "Really, Graham. Come on."

He smiled and leaned into me. It was one of those incomplete, sloppy smiles; he'd definitely had a lot to drink. "Okay, they aren't your biggest fans but—I think they're wrong."

"It's fine. You should hate me, too, really. I don't know how you don't."

I didn't want him to hate me, but how could he not? I'd destroyed him.

Graham grew quiet and ran a hand through his hair. "I did. For a while."

"What changed?" I whispered.

He shrugged. Wrong question, I guess. "You're Gonna Make Me When You Go" seeped outside through the cracks. I could only hear the irony. Did he hear it too? Graham looked at me as the song played and neither of us moved, stuck in that moment between so much to say and no clue how to say it. Between wanting to touch him and wanting to run away.

Graham's fingers grazed my cheek, and my stomach folded in on itself. At least that's how it felt. Like I was falling. He pulled his hand away quickly. "Anyway, sorry for tonight. I really don't hate you, Cassie. They just don't want me to get hurt."

They think I will hurt him, like before. Maybe they're right to think that.

I nodded. "Goodnight, Graham."

He surprised me by hugging me. Graham squeezed me tight, and the full length of my body was pressed against him. His arms held me closer, and every cell tingled. I wanted to stay there close to him. I wanted so much more, and he was right there. It wouldn't take much to have it again, to lean in and close the space between us.

He pulled away. It was probably best since he'd been drinking and I was obviously out of my mind.

Graham went the rest of the way down the steps, and then turned to me again. His eyes were dark. "Tell me one thing: were you happy? After you left, were you happy?"

"No," I said, not even stopping to think about what that meant for him. But I thought I could be. I wanted to be. When I found out about my dad, I thought if I left and started over then I could ignore it all. All it did was make it worse.

He nodded slowly, and looked away from me. I could tell it wasn't the answer he wanted by the way his whole body tensed. I wished I had been happy after I left. Part of me knew he wished the same because even though I hurt him, he'd always wanted me to be happy. It was all he'd ever wanted, except he'd always thought it would be him to make me happy. Maybe it could be, someday.

"I think I could be, though. Someday," I said. It was low, but he heard me because he looked at me again. The music played around us and I knew that I meant it. Whatever I went to Indiana searching for, I hadn't found. Maybe it had always been missing. Or maybe it had always been right here and I hadn't seen it.

"What will it take for you to get there?" Graham asked.

What would it take? I wanted to say it was him. That before I left, he had made me happy. He was the only bright spot in my life, and that was terrifying. I wanted to say that he was right, that my mom was right, and I had come home a little for him. Probably more so than I even knew, but I couldn't. I couldn't do that to him when he was someone else's. Someone who wouldn't break him.

"I don't know," I said.

Graham nodded. "I hope you find it."

24.

Graham

I PUT THE key in the ignition. I had twenty-five minutes to pick up Molly and get us to Hixton's Corner for brunch with her aunt. I'd never even met her aunt, and that wasn't how I wanted to spend my Saturday morning. My head was pounding; I guessed I drank more than I realized. If not for the three texts from Molly, I probably would've forgotten all about brunch. I barely remembered it, but when I thought really hard it was in the back of my head, vaguely—right next to the vibrant image of Cass in that green dress last night. The way she looked with her hair like that and her jacket and her eyes sparkling.

I shook my head and rolled down the window so the sun could hit my skin and wake me up. It was bright outside. We had a hot summer ahead. I started to back out of the spot when Cassie's voice floated to my ears. I froze there for a second, glancing at my mirror while she sat outside on the porch. I waited to see what she would do, but she was still and silent, staring over the horizon. I don't know if she saw me, but she didn't look my way.

I kept seeing her like she was last night. Not before dinner when she looked beautiful or during when she looked uncomfortable. But after. When I stood on her porch and asked her if she was happy.

There was something in her eyes, something written on her face, that seemed hopeful. Something that seemed like she knew there could be something to make her happy, but she didn't know how to say it. Or if she wanted to. Like breathing its name would burst the dream. I felt it between us in the air, that hope.

Music started and Mrs. H yelled, "I love this song!" I was too far away to make out the lyrics, but I strained my ear to listen. I wanted to hear it, to be part of a moment with them like I used to be. Even for a second.

What are you doing? Go get Molly.

I put the truck in drive and started down the street, but even when I turned the corner, I still felt that hope. It was the last thing I expected to feel last night, the last thing I understood, but I knew it was mine as much as it was hers.

MOLLY KISSED ME as she got into my truck and she smelled like vanilla. It was making my hangover worse. *Don't vomit.* That was all I could think about.

"Aunt Kat's really excited to meet you," Molly said, her fingers on my shoulder as we drove.

I nodded. "I'm sure it will be great."

"How was last night?"

In my mind, I see Cass's face when she saw me in the parking lot. The way her hand bumped mine while we walked. She never smelled like vanilla that made my head spin.

"Fine," I said. It wasn't really fine. Not at the end. That conversation with her had me so confused. She left to be happy and she wasn't, so why did she stay away?

Stop thinking about Cassie.

Stop caring. I needed to stop caring. To stop worrying about her family, to stop listening to her music. To stop wanting to be in her moments because I wasn't in her life. I'd been down that road and I knew where it ended. I needed to clear my head.

I took a deep breath and cringed at the overwhelming scent of vanilla.

"Are you even listening to me?" Molly asked, poking my shoulder.

I parked the car. "What?"

She huffed and crossed her arms. "You weren't even listening. Where is your head today? The whole way here you've been somewhere else."

My head was in places it shouldn't have been. I knew that, but I couldn't keep it grounded. I couldn't focus on Molly when I kept hearing Cass's laugh, and seeing her smile, and listening to her pronounce every word like it was the most important thing I had ever heard.

What was happening to me?

I knew what was happening. This was the same way it felt when I was fifteen and I wanted to kiss her for the first time. This was how it was before I fell the first time.

Molly stared at me, arms across her chest.

"What?" I asked.

"Seriously?" she yelled. Molly jerked the door open and stormed around the front of the truck. Her blonde head bobbed in front of me and I jumped out too.

"Sorry," I said, pulling at her arm until she stopped walking. "I'm tired. I drank too much last night."

Even saying that made me feel like an ass. Maybe *all* of this was because I drank too much. I didn't have any feelings for Cass. Last night was an illusion, a haze of alcohol. Cassie was a friend, kind of, and that was all. Molly was my girlfriend. Cass was my past; Molly was now.

"I'm really sorry," I said.

"Is something else going on that we need—"

I shook my head. "I'm really looking forward to meeting your aunt."

Molly raised an eyebrow. "You're sure? You don't have to do this."

"I'm sure," I said, taking her hand.

She smiled, and I knew this was where I needed to be. Molly was solid and real. I never had to wonder what she was thinking because she told me. We were still getting to know each other, instead of hiding pieces. She knew how to surprise me, how to live life unafraid. She'd spent the last few months showing me what I really wanted and helping me reach out to grab it. That was the truth, and truth was stronger than hope.

25.

Cassie

THIS OFFICE STILL looked the same as it had the first time I met Dr. Lambert four years ago, back when we found out Mom was bipolar. I crossed my legs, uncrossed them, and rested my hands at my side. Next to my seat was a side table covered in little random items. Rubber bands, stress balls, little toys, a Zen sand garden with a mini rake thing. I debated picking one up, but settled on the pillow and clung for dear life as the door closed.

"Thanks for coming, Cassie."

I looked around the office, and followed Dr. Lambert's movement. "Why am I here again?"

Dr. Lambert grabbed a pen, and sat across from me with a smile. "Joyce and I have been speaking a lot about how all this has affected you. She told me a little about your discussion with her a few weeks ago."

I shifted in the seat. "Discussion?"

"The one when you tried to get her to take her meds and recounted a few of your childhood disappointments."

Mom told her all that? "Was I not supposed to say

that to her?"

Dr. Lambert crossed her legs in her chair. "On the contrary. Cassie, no one knows your mother's illness better than you. You're the one who is best suited to help her."

"I can help her?"

She focused her eyes on me. Therapists were amazing with the way they could zoom in, like they found that one flaw on perfect skin and made a target out of it. It was unsettling. "The next time I saw her that moment was all she could talk about. She didn't know about all of those moments, not consciously, not in a way that meant anything to her. Part of her recovery, part of her journey to self-sufficiency depends on you being honest with her, on being vulnerable."

I wanted to laugh because that wasn't something I did well. "Self-sufficiency?"

"Bipolar disorder isn't the end of a life; it's the beginning of a new one. Joyce has the capability to take care of herself, to be on her meds, to work if she wants, but she lacks currently the drive and the understanding. That's our job. Yours and mine."

Our job. The only real team I'd ever been on was with Graham. He'd said "we" a lot. Eventually, it did feel like we until eventually we weren't. Now we were on opposite teams or even different games, maybe. I grabbed a small squishy ball from the table and squeezed it in my hands.

"So what—you want me to tell Mom all the ways she's disappointed me? That doesn't seem helpful."

"Not exactly," Dr. Lambert said. "I want you and I to have a discussion right now, that's all. I want you to tell me about yourself."

I dropped the ball back down. This whole table next to my seat was an arsenal for avoidance. "You know me."

"I used to, but you're not the same girl who visited me in this office a year ago. Are you?"

I laughed and squeezed the pillow. "I definitely am not."

"So, tell me who you are. Tell me something real," she said, uncrossing her legs. I tried to find somewhere to focus on in the room. Somewhere not Dr. Lambert. Something real about myself. I wrapped my finger around a frayed thread dangling from the pillow. "You're nervous?"

"I don't really talk about myself much at school. I'm a little out of practice."

"Why don't you talk about yourself?"

I shrugged. "I went there to reinvent myself."

"To change?"

I nodded. "I left everything because I thought I could escape who I was there, who my mom was, what her past was. I wanted to be happy."

Dr. Lambert clicked her pen, but she didn't write anything down. She didn't look away from me in case moving her gaze meant I would disappear completely. "I remember that you were conflicted, unsure, a little stressed. You never mentioned anything about happiness. You weren't happy here?"

"I was."

"But you wanted a different happiness? What were you really trying to find?"

"I wanted to stop it from repeating."

"Stop what from repeating?"

I stared at Dr. Lambert. Her eyes were wide and brown, open like she really did care. I took a breath and picked up one of the rubber bands off the table, wrapping it around my fingers. I didn't look up at her, just watched the green band twist around my fingertips.

"I was five and we spent all day in the car. I remember the metal seatbelt was hot on my skin because she didn't like to use the air conditioning. Mom always preferred the purity of the wind. 'Everything in its natural state.' Before we went, she bought me this set of brand new crayons and a unicorn coloring book. The picture I remember the most had a unicorn trying to eat the moon, and I colored it pink," I said. I was already smiling at the memory. I hadn't thought about that day in so long, but I could recall a lot of details. "All day we were in the car. It was hot, I was hungry and Mom told me, 'It will all be worth it when we get there, Cassie. You have to wait for good things.' We ended up at the beach in Wilmington. It's like a four-hour drive and when we got there I cried because I didn't want to get out and she made me anyway, dragged me through the parking lot while I was screaming."

The rubber band stretched as I pulled it across both my hands. I had to focus on it. I didn't want to see her face. I didn't want to see pity there, or something worse.

"But then we got closer and I saw these lights from this Ferris wheel. The whole boardwalk was a carnival with rides and games and food. She knelt down, a big smile on her face, and wiped my eyes. 'You want to have some fun?' I remember everything about that day. I won a stuffed mouse that was white with a red-and-white lollipop and floppy ears, which is still in my bedroom. We played games, ate lots of food. At the end of the day, there was a concert once the sun set. I have no idea who they were. I just remember her singing, swaying with me on her hip, and me playing with this glow stick necklace she got me. I fell asleep on the ride home."

"That doesn't seem like a bad moment."

"It wasn't," I said, unwinding the rubber band from my fingers. "But it was her first manic episode—at least the one I can remember. The next day she was still chipper, so happy and cheerful. We went shopping. Everything was smiles and sunshine and presents and adventures."

"For how long?"

I shrugged, sliding the band on my wrist. "Five days. Five days my mom was the most excited, the most cheerful, the most amazing. I said to her that second day, 'Mommy, you're pretty today.' And she said, 'You're pretty, too. It's a pretty day!' That's what we called them before we knew that's what they were, her manic episodes. They were pretty days."

"And then they weren't?"

I nodded. "And then they weren't." I threw the rubber band back on the table and let my gaze drift back to Dr. Lambert's face. She was still watching me, notepad and pen in her hand, but she wasn't writing.

I readjusted how I was sitting, pulled my legs up into the couch and kept ahold of that pillow. "She was always more hypomanic in the beginning—happy, reckless, excited. She would talk fast or get an idea in her head and we had to do it. Right then. A few times I would wake up at night and she would be in the middle of an episode and I'd hear it."

"Hear what?"

I closed my eyes quickly, exhaled. "Her in her bedroom having sex with whatever guy she'd found. I don't know where they came from, but they were around in the beginning a lot more than when I was older. Or maybe she didn't bring them home. I don't know."

She scribbled something on her notebook. After

a second, she met my gaze. "The majority of bipolar patients suffer from depressive episodes. Do you remember her first depressive episodes that affected you?"

The first one I thought of was the night I left Graham. I didn't want to share that one.

I cleared my throat. I knew the statistics and the general cases. Long states of depression, then manic highs.

"My mom was more like a tsunami. For months, she'd be fine. She'd be herself. Then all of a sudden she'd be in my face like a bee drawn to sugar. Adventure was sugar. Shopping was the sugar. That's how we got the convertible—on a manic episode when I was eleven."

I remembered that day too. She'd just received a check for one of the songs she produced. She cashed that whole check on the car.

"I really only remember one time vividly that was early on," I said.

"Tell me about it."

I stared beyond Dr. Lambert, studying the lines on the wallpaper. They swirled and cascaded into each other until I couldn't tell them apart.

"When I was eleven it snowed," I started. That storm was a big deal, because it rarely snowed in our part of North Carolina—and never like that. "Everything was white and it was so deep it was above my knees. I wanted to play outside, but Graham wasn't answering the phone. We were the only two kids our age on our street, but Mom made me French toast and played The Beatles all morning, and she was happy."

I remember thinking how much she must've loved snow, with that look on her face.

"I told Mom I wanted to build a fort. She asked if I

knew how, but I didn't, and she grinned and said she did." I smiled a little at the memory. Mom put on as many layers as she could find, since we didn't have much real outside wear, and tied bread bags over my socks before I'd put my rain boots on. She'd held my hand as we walked through the snow. I'd loved her like that and I'd never wanted her to let go.

"We made a snowman and had a snowball fight and made a fort from the trashcans around the back of our house. We must have been out there for hours because I remember everything hurt, frozen, but I didn't care. It was beautiful and Mom was happy and everything was amazing," I said with a pause.

I looked at Dr. Lambert from the corner of my eye, and she listened, intensely. Her face showed no emotion, and I didn't know how someone heard a story and showed no emotion. I cleared my throat.

"Then Mom showed me how to make a snow angel. 'Count to twenty and come find me. If you find me, we'll have cocoa.' She snuck around the corner and I laughed and made that angel.

"I didn't stop. I moved my arms and legs like she showed me, and stared up at the sky as flakes started to fall again and counted as loud as I could. When I hit twenty I stood up carefully so I didn't mess up my angel."

It was quiet in the room, just like it had been that day.

"There were no tracks anymore because the snow was coming down hard, so I couldn't find her. I went the way I saw her go, but the whole world was frozen and covered in white. It was still and quiet. I called her name, over and over. It felt like forever as I searched for her, behind everything, under everything. I didn't know where she went. I cried."

I continued talking because if I stopped, even for a breath, I wouldn't be able to start again. "I walked to the woods. Mom wouldn't go in there, but I walked along the edge of the woods anyway. I found her curled up at the spot near the fence where the woods and the grass met, sobbing on the ground. I thought she was hurt, but she started rambling about being sorry, about hating everything, and I knew she was lost. I tried to get her inside, but she couldn't even hear me. When she was like that, she never really registered that I was around."

I remembered the whole thing like yesterday. The cold. The weight of her. Trying to drag her through the snow.

"Every other step she would fall down and start bawling over again. She would call out for my dad— Richard—like he was around the corner waiting. 'He's inside,' I kept telling her. 'We have to get inside.' And that's when Graham came outside."

"Graham saw you with her in that state?" Dr. Lambert asked.

I nodded and shifted in my seat. His face when he saw us there was confused and concerned. I'd told him I couldn't get her inside. The wind pierced my skin and I couldn't feel my legs or arms. Graham asked me if she was hurt.

"She's sad," I'd said.

"Does she get sad a lot?"

"Can you help me?"

"I'm sure my dad can—"

"No!" I'd yelled at him. He'd looked scared. "You have to help me. You can't tell anyone. Promise me forever. You will not tell anyone ever."

His eyebrows furrowed, but he'd nodded. "Promise, forever."

Dr. Lambert said my name. "Cassie, what did Graham do?"

"He helped me get her inside. Somehow we convinced her to walk, but when we got into the house she collapsed on the couch. Graham stood in the kitchen and watched me. He didn't say anything until I sat down at the table and I made him promise not to tell."

Dr. Lambert's forehead creased as she wrote down a couple notes. "He kept that promise. We didn't find out about Joyce for four more years."

I locked eyes with her. "Graham always keeps his promises."

"Do you remember any other signs?"

There were probably more, statistically. I knew it was common for kids to build a tolerance, to block out the things they didn't want to remember. Maybe I did that.

"She slept a lot sometimes. There was a whole week where I don't remember seeing her and we didn't have food in the house because she couldn't get out of bed. I took myself to school; I made her breakfast that she didn't eat. I ate at the Tuckers' house every meal that week and told Mrs. Tucker that Mom was sick."

Dr. Lambert nodded. "Mrs. Tucker knew?"

"Maybe. I don't know. She was always really careful what she said around me, and then when we found Mom in the bathtub a few years later—well, then there was no denying it."

"Let's talk about that."

"About what?" I snapped. I didn't want to talk about finding Mom. That was the worst experience, and I've had to live it over and over for four years. No way I was going there.

"The denial," she said. I exhaled. "You made Graham

137

promise when you were eleven not to tell anyone. How long did that last?"

I wracked my brain. "I guess until I was fifteen, when I found her in the bathtub, when I found out she was bipolar."

"For four years he kept your secret," she said with a pause. She clicked her pen closed. "Why didn't you want anyone to know? You could've had someone help you. A lot of your heartbreak could have been prevented."

When she put it like that, it sucked. I was a kid. How was I supposed to know? I squeezed the pillow into my chest.

"I knew it wasn't normal compared to other people, but it was all I knew. She was my mom. That life. Mom being happy; Mom being sad—it was mine," I said. I looked right at Dr. Lambert when I spoke. "It had always been mine. In middle school I realized it wasn't normal, but by then I knew that if I said anything I could lose her; I could be taken away and I didn't want that. She was all I had. She was my mom." I didn't want to lose her. "There were days when she wasn't sick, when she was normal. Those were *really* the pretty ones. The ones I want to remember most, and I can't because of the rest."

Dr. Lambert leaned forward in her chair. "You said you wanted to stop it from repeating. What exactly did you mean?"

I threw the pillow down. "I don't want to ever have anyone else feel that way about me."

"What way?"

My throat tightened. "I don't want them to remember what I did, the bad things, and forget me. I don't want anyone to suffer because of me. If I end up like her." I picked the pillow back up. "So I didn't tell anyone at college about Mom or this place or Graham. I went and tried to start over."

"That was hard?"

"Very hard. I had a friend, June, and a boyfriend, but they weren't real. They were the 'After Cassie.'"

"After? After what?"

I wanted to stand up. I wanted to run, but I knew I couldn't do that. I let a silence settle around us until I couldn't handle the lack of noise. I reached for this bendy blue straw thing on the table. "Before I left Graham, I found Mom in a manic state. She was yelling about my dad, and she told me—she didn't know I was Cassie—that he left because of her. And I snooped around. I found their divorce papers. 'After Cassie' is after Mom told me about my dad. After I left Graham to go there. After everything."

It was the last thing I expected to find, but it was nestled in the trunk near the foot of her bed right beside my birth certificate. My dad wasn't dead; he was alive. The reason for their divorce was listed as "emotional stress and turmoil." He left because he couldn't handle her emotional trials. He left because she was sick.

"Why did you leave Graham?"

Dr. Lambert rested in the back of her chair, studying me, legs crossed. I looked at her because I wanted her to hear this part too. I wanted this part to matter, because this part was the stuff that made me After Cassie. She'd said I'd changed, and I had. "I didn't want to hurt him, to trap him in a life with me. I didn't think I could stand it if he left me like that. I didn't let anyone at Butler get close to me."

"Why?"

A simple question; a complicated answer. I grabbed the blue bendy straw and twisted it into an O before I answered. "I don't want to be abandoned the way my mom was."

"The way your father left?"

"Yes," I said.

"The way you left Graham?"

My eyes shot up. That made it sound so easy. It wasn't easy. None of it had been. I followed her row of degrees until my eyes met the windowsill. The sun seeped through a crack in the blinds.

"The way I left her, too," I said. "I'd rather do the leaving."

"But does the leaving make you happier than staying?"

"No," I said in barely a whisper.

"Thank you," Dr. Lambert said.

"For what?" I asked, looking at her again.

"For telling me something real," she said. I froze, bendy straw in one hand, pillow pressed against me. It did feel simple. Suddenly. My complicated life. My messy emotions. Simple. "Cassie, I think it would be good for you to keep seeing me. If you want to."

"I don't need any help."

"Everyone needs help, Cassie. Besides, I think you know that's not true."

"Dr. Lambert—"

She didn't let me finish. She threw the notebook and the pen on the table beside her. "I think you need to let someone in. You need someone to talk to, and it doesn't mean you're sick or crazy. We're human. We're wired to need other humans. To share, to talk, to trust. I want to be that person for you, Cassie, until you're ready for it to be someone else. We can talk about anything you want, but I think it would help you."

"Help me what?"

"Exactly," she said.

26.

Graham

I CHECKED MY phone as I turned on the shower after my Wednesday morning run. Three emails. I stopped taking the thing with me a long time ago. For some reason the universe knew when I was trying to exercise and everyone needed something in that hour. I didn't listen to music, anyway. I liked the sound of my breathing, my heartbeat in my head, nature and traffic and animals. It kept me moving forward, pushed me on.

The third email made me freeze. It was from Rice University saying my status had been updated. Holy shit. Was this it? My hands shook as I logged into my account. I had to try twice because I kept pushing the wrong letters. Stupid fucking touchscreen phones. The page loaded and I clicked on my account.

Where the screen usually said, "Waiting," it said, "Approved."

Approved.

Approved.

What a great fucking word.

I clicked on the link below the Best Word and directions popped up. I was officially an entering junior at Rice University in the architecture program. Classes started in late August. It went on to talk about payment, housing, forms, a bunch of shit I didn't care about right then because I was accepted. I was going to Texas. I was going to school. I did it. I fucking did it!

∞◯ᘓ

"MOM!" I YELLED, busting into the kitchen. She was sitting at the table eating breakfast and probably reading some romance novel on her e-reader when she looked up at me. I smiled, like a crazy idiot probably, but I didn't care. I was going to school!

"What's going on, Graham?" she asked, taking a bite of her eggs.

I leaned back against the kitchen counter. I could play this cool. "I was wondering what you were doing in August?"

Mom shook her head and took another bite. "How am I supposed to know that? I don't know. Nothing?"

"Good—because we have to go to Texas to take me to school."

Her fork froze mid-air. "What?"

I smiled. "Rice starts in August. I have to be there the twenty-fifth. If you want to put it in your calendar."

She dropped her fork. "You got in?"

"I got in!"

Mom cheered, and jumped up from her seat. She wasn't disapproving when I decided to stay here after graduation. I told her I was trying to figure it out, but really, it had been for Cassie. But this, she knew how much I wanted it. She wanted it for me. Mom laughed, stretched her arms up around my neck to hug me.

"I have to call your father! We'll plan a dinner when your dad is back in town!" She kissed my cheek and left me in the kitchen. I could hear her still cheering, still excited, from across the house.

I had to go tell Molly. I knew she was at work, so I was almost to my truck when Joyce called my name. I debated getting in my truck anyway and walking on like I hadn't heard her, but then I'd already paused. Now it would be rude. Besides, I wasn't mad at her. I wasn't mad at anyone. I was moving on, officially now, and that was allowed.

"Graham," Mrs. H said, a smile on her face. "Good morning."

"That it is, Mrs. H."

"I know it's short notice, Graham, but we are having game night tonight. Remember how we used to do that every month?" she asked.

I nodded. I'd remembered. One night a month in high school Mrs. H had game night for Cassie and our gang. It was after she got on her meds when she was more stable. We'd all come over and hang out with Cassie. She'd give us all a beer and play some kind of great music in the background, and we'd make up our own rules to whatever we were playing.

"You're invited, if you can come," she said.

I shook my head. "I would, Mrs. H, but I have plans with my girlfriend. We're celebrating tonight." I didn't have plans yet, but I would. She'd be excited for me. She wanted this for me almost as much as I did.

"Celebrating what?"

"I was accepted into a college I really wanted," I said.

"Oh, you got into Rice?"

"You remember that?"

She smiled. "I remember a lot, Graham Tucker. I'm bipolar, not old." I chuckled, even though she was both things. "You have fun with your girlfriend, but we'll have to do it another time. I want to celebrate with you, and I'm sure Cassie will too."

"Yes ma'am," I said.

I sent Molly a text that I was coming to visit her. Her response was quick: **I am sick.** She was sick.

Do you want me to come by?

No. Not pretty :(

Feel better.

I slid my phone away. *Crap.* I turned back to the Harlen house. I knew I shouldn't go there, but it was like nothing else was listening as my feet led me there. I could have game night with them. I could hang out with Cassie if I wanted to. I didn't want to be with her. I knew I was where I was supposed to be with Molly, and then I was supposed to go to Texas. I could do this. We could be friends, really friends. Not some other form that didn't feel right.

And besides, I could get out at any time.

Mrs. H answered the door. "Actually, game night sounds wonderful."

27.

Cassie

GRAHAM LAUGHED. IT was the best sound. Each time it echoed through my house, it shook something inside me. It was just the three of us, and playing Life didn't really scream party, but there was something about us sitting here and Cheap Trick playing around us. The last two months had been good for me. Being here, with them, sparked something I'd lost in Indiana. I'd been more like myself since I'd been home. Mom did that; Graham did that.

The doorbell rang and all three of us shared a glance.

"I want the green piece!" I called, and went to the door to get the pizza. We ordered Graham's favorite to celebrate his big news. Mom even made him a cake. When I opened the door, there was no pizza.

There was a girl. With a mess of short brown and purple curls, a cigarette resting in the corner of her mouth and standing with a closed, dripping yellow umbrella. She had a suitcase beside her.

"June," I said. What the hell was June doing on my

porch? I didn't know she was coming. She was pissed. I was happy to see her, but not. Inside, they were laughing again. How would I explain them to her? I stepped onto the porch. "What are you doing here?"

"I told you not to disappear," she said.

"I didn't."

She huffed, took a long drag of her cigarette, and crossed her arms. "It's been a month since we talked. You haven't answered my emails or called me back. Friends don't disappear like that without a word—so I came for a visit."

I hadn't been sure what to say to her, so I'd ignored her. It was wrong, but I didn't think she'd come here. "How did you even get this address?"

"Pete Langley snuck me into admissions during finals—just in case. I would've called, but I didn't think you'd answer. So I thought, 'I'll go down there and see what's keeping her so busy she can't talk to her best friend.' And here I am."

"Cass? Everything okay with the pizza?" Graham asked. I reached for the door, but he was quicker and he opened it. June's eyes widened with the door, and she took another drag off her cigarette. This was awkward. Graham looked at her suitcase, and then at me. "Hi," he said.

"June, this is Graham. Graham, June."

"Pleasure," June said.

"Same," he said with a pause. "Cassie didn't mention you were coming?"

"It was a surprise," she said. I tossed her an annoyed look when she emphasized the last word. She was smiling, though, like she'd done it intentionally.

Graham smirked, and I could tell he was gloating too. Great. They were already teaming up. "I'll leave you two alone."

He went back inside, and June threw her cigarette to the ground. I watched as it soaked up the rain and went out. "Wow, he's hot. No wonder you haven't called me back! I bet he keeps you busy, big boy like that." I blushed; I could feel it on my cheeks. "Is he yours?"

"No," I said.

"I'll take him," she said, looking over my shoulder through the little crack in the door.

"He's taken," I said.

June raised her eyebrows only for a second before nodding. "He's the one from before?" I didn't answer. June didn't know about Graham, but she'd known about a boy I left behind. The one who made me boy-sick. "That's a story I'm going to hear later, right?"

I shrugged and glanced at her suitcase. She was definitely planning to stay, then.

"Are we going to go inside now or do I need to light another cigarette to keep myself warm?

I reached out for her bag. "We're about to play Life."

"Can I be yellow?"

"Sure," I said. June hugged me before we went inside.

29.

Graham

CASSIE SMILED A lot when June was around. It was almost as if she brought out this part of Cass that was hidden. I couldn't stop staring at her. That smile was too perfect. God, I was an idiot. I should've left too, run away. Fast and far, like she had. I thought I could do this, but being around her made it harder.

I wasn't as strong as I thought. I already felt myself slipping into her grasp. Into that same web that I lived in for ten years where Cassie was everything. Where I was content as long as I was with her. I told myself I could get out at any time, but part of me knew better than believing it.

"How long will you be staying with us, June?" Mrs. H asked.

June smiled and grabbed a slice of pizza. "As long as I'm welcome. I hadn't really planned this trip. I'm more of a play-it-by-ear kind of girl."

"Me too," Mrs. H said in reply. "You're welcome here as long as you want to stay. Any friend of Cassie's."

Cassie shifted awkwardly and I wondered what

she was thinking. And then I wondered if I would ever be able to stop wondering that.

"How long have you known Cassie?" June asked me before she took a bite of her pizza.

I met Cassie's gaze across the living room. I hadn't realized she'd been looking at me, but now that our eyes were locked on each other, I could almost feel that she was. She was still smiling, and the memory of the first time I saw her replayed in my head. It's crazy how something that happened forever ago felt just like yesterday. "She stormed into my life when I was nine."

"I think you stormed into mine. I lived here first."

"I was never the storm," I said. Cassie's smile fell, but her eyes didn't leave mine. Staring at her like that made my head feel like it was floating, and like she was the only thing I could see clearly. And she was mesmerizing. The curves of her face were my anchor, and the light freckles on her nose were my sun, and her lips were the key to every secret in the universe. I wanted everything. To know it all again like I had before she left, but to explore it all with the Cassie that sat across from me.

Cassie looked away from me. Her eyes darted toward the ground, and I shook away the feeling. I refocused. I couldn't stare at her like that. Couldn't think about her that way. What was I doing here? This was stupid. I was stupid.

"Childhood sweethearts?" June asked. Cassie sent her dagger eyes, but June didn't seem like the type to be swayed by Cassie's looks. That was a rare thing.

Childhood everything.

"Something like that," I said. I had to change this conversation. Talking about what we were before wasn't going to help anything. "How did you meet Cassie?"

June leaned back on the couch. "Ah, she was hiding in the corner at early admission orientation. I was drawn to her."

"She does that," I said.

Both of those things, hiding and drawing people toward her. I looked at her, and Cassie was already staring at me again. With her eyes on me, I had the sudden urge to kiss her. To move across the room and pull her up and surprise her with a kiss that held everything I felt. To hell with who was watching us. Would that kiss be the same as it used to be? Would it, like us, still fit so perfectly as it did a year ago? Would it be more? Tornadoes and hurricanes that had been held at bay for a year? Or had that changed as much as we both had?

My eyes drifted to her lips, and I saw her breath hitch too. I wanted it. Her. I wanted Cass. I wanted her so much that it was hard to think, hard to breathe, like all the air had been sucked out of the room.

I had to get out of there. I stood up quickly, knocking a glass of water to the floor. Mrs. H yelled that she had it, and disappeared into the kitchen. I couldn't be thinking about kissing Cassie. I had to run.

"Sorry—I remembered I have a thing. I should go," I said.

I slammed the door on my way out.

30.

Cassie

JUNE AND I pulled up outside of Dr. Lambert's office. It was a bright morning. Perfect for playing tourist of our little town for a couple hours.

"Where are you going?" Mom asked as she got out of the car.

"I'm giving her the whole Lumberton experience."

"Start with ice cream," she said, closing the door. Even though she couldn't see me, I nodded.

"Bye, Mrs. H!" June yelled as Mom crossed the street. June already liked Mom. She spent all day yesterday telling stories from her time in the music business. When Mom told June she once met June Carter Cash, I knew she was hooked forever. My mother could do that to people.

I tapped the steering wheel. "So, what caused your impromptu visit? Aside from my crappiness as a friend."

"I need a reason?" June asked, gathering her hair up into a ponytail.

I shook my head. "No, but I think there is one. It's

been three days and you haven't mentioned Jason at all."

She groaned. "Jason and I broke up. He's in Florida; I'm wherever. It was too complicated. He was too clingy. I don't screw clingy boys."

"June, you are a treasure. I don't know how anyone let you go."

"I don't either!" she yelled with a smile. "Where are we going?"

"Only the best ice cream parlor in North Carolina."

"At 10 in the morning?"

"Are you objecting?" I asked.

"To ice cream? Never. I was clarifying."

Having June here was nice. We hadn't talked about any of the other stuff, the real stuff, but with her, it was easy. It was fun. She made me feel like it was possible to be more than where you came from. I knew her story. I knew about her alcoholic mother and her drug-dealing father. I knew about her life in Los Angeles and her time in and out of foster care, and I knew that she had overcome that. June was her own person; she was strong, and being around her made me feel like I could be the same. She was probably the best thing that happened to me at Butler, even though having her at my house was a little weird.

June reached out and changed the radio station. Some poppy country song thing played in my speakers. I groaned.

"I don't listen to that stuff," I said, reaching out to turn it off.

"Harlen, chill. Don't be a music snob."

"But I *am* a music snob."

"Branch out a little. Take a breath. I promise, it won't kill you to listen to something from this decade. Or the last one. I seriously don't know how you grew up without boy bands and pop princesses," she said.

I shuddered. "You don't know that it couldn't kill me. Bad music could very well kill me."

She chuckled. "Don't be a diva."

"I'm not a diva."

"You *totally* are a diva."

I rolled my eyes. "Driver picks the music."

"Not this time, Harlen. Not this time." She stuck her tongue out at me. We were almost there anyway, so it didn't matter. I could block out this crap for a few minutes.

The poppy-country song ended and the radio station transitioned into something darker. A smooth melody with a sharp edge started, and I perked up. There was something about this that sounded raw already.

"Oh my God, this song," June started, reaching for the radio. "I'll turn it off."

I swatted her hand away. "Why would you turn it off? It might not suck like everything else."

"You don't know this song?" June asked, her voice getting higher.

"Know it? Why would I know it?"

She released this laugh-squeal thing. "Wait—you don't know? You really don't know? Is North Carolina a black hole?"

She was acting so strange. Even for June. I looked at her; her jaw dropped and her eyes were wide. "Know what?"

The opening lyrics started and my skin tingled. I knew that voice. That rough, deep, scratchy voice. As soon as the line started, this pit formed in my stomach. I listened closer, because there was no way.

I woke up and you were gone // I should've known it all along // From that far-off look in your eyes // And the smile that never stretched to the sides // Your mouth was mine, but your heart was stone // And I tried to reach it, to break it down // No matter what I did you couldn't be found

I glanced over at June, and the way her brow furrowed told me it was true. That was Rohan.

But now you're gone, gone, gone // Every memory I had is wrong, wrong, wrong // You left without a word // You're gone, gone, gone // You didn't have the nerve to say // Goodbye / But I should've known from the look in your eye // You're gone, gone, gone.

I closed my eyes. This wasn't happening. This could be about anyone.

The only thing I have left of you // Is a memory of your head on my chest // And the goodbye you wrote on the back of my chemistry test

Or it's totally me. June flipped off the radio before the song ended, and my hands were frozen on the steering wheel in the parking lot of the ice cream shop, and my brain was reeling. Rohan was on the radio. He wrote a song about me. I broke his heart.

June cleared her throat. "Surprise?" What was that? I didn't even know what had just happened. "It came out last week."

"How?" Rohan was on the radio.

"I told you they had a label interested, and when they played this song the label had to have them."

"It doesn't happen that fast!"

"Apparently it can," she said. "They're going on tour for the whole summer."

"Wow," I said. Rohan did it. He was on his way to getting his dreams.

"Yeah," she said. "Intense. Was that how it happened? On the back of his chemistry test?"

I nodded. June didn't say anything about it, but she

didn't need to. I knew I was horrible. I knew it was.

"Let's get that ice cream," June said, jumping out of the car. I followed her out even though the last thing I wanted was ice cream.

WE TURNED LEFT on the sidewalk a few feet from the ice cream parlor, but my mind was still on Rohan's song. I had no idea he felt anything serious for me. How much of those lyrics were really his feelings? We'd only been together six months, and only seriously for three of them. The first three were that exploration of the new and exciting. It was never serious, at least I never thought. Then, I went to see his band play and he introduced me as his girlfriend. Then, we were that. Girlfriend, boyfriend—at least something to that extent. There was never a discussion. There were never any "L" words exchanged or conversations about feelings or expectations. I didn't know leaving would break his heart, too.

"It's okay," June said, staring at me as we walked. I glanced over to meet her gaze. "It's going to be okay, Cassie."

"I know," I said, but I didn't. My mind flickered back to Dr. Lambert's office last week. Was I so scared of being abandoned that I left everyone else? That I didn't let anyone in? Even June didn't know what I didn't want her to see.

June elbowed me, and when I glanced up we were face-to-face with Graham.

I inhaled sharply. Perfect. This was perfect. My heart was already falling to pieces, so now, the universe was going to crush them.

"Hey," Graham said. He looked between the two of us, and I stopped moving. His whole presence set me on edge, and his eyes focused in on me. I didn't want him to look, because I knew he would see that I was upset.

"Hey," I said back. Wordlessly, he used his free hand to fix that piece of hair in my face, and his finger lingered on my cheek. I felt myself on the brink of losing it when he pulled his hand away.

"We were getting ice cream," June said suddenly. She pointed to the store and bumped me on the shoulder. She gave me a weird look. "Cassie said this was the best place in the state."

"It is; you'll love it," Graham said without looking away from me. His expression went from happy to concerned. "You okay?" he asked.

I nodded, even though I was far from it. I didn't want him to ask me anything, because if he didn't ask then I didn't have to lie or worse, tell him the truth. But then I wanted him to ask. I wanted to tell him and let him hold me and forgive me and tell me it was going to be all right. I needed him, and I wanted him, and I wished I didn't feel either.

We stared at each other and he knew I was lying. I could see it in the way his eyes narrowed in on me, and the way he nodded slowly. I couldn't tell him about this; it would not end in a good way for us.

"How's your visit been?" Graham asked June, finally looking away from me.

"Great. Cassie always knows how to provide the best entertainment."

I raised my eyebrows at June, but she flashed a big smile. I tried not to look back at Graham. Not to be unnerved by him because I was close to losing it. I couldn't lose it in front of Graham.

"You want to join us for ice cream?" June asked, her eyes wide as she looked between us.

Graham shifted on his feet, and I looked at him again. *Say yes.* The air between us felt frozen, waiting for something to happen. He was a magnet and my eyes were stuck there on his face. On the sharp cut of his jaw, and the piercing grey of his eyes, and the concern edging on his cheeks. I knew if he stayed he'd get the truth out of me, and part of me felt like that was a good thing. I could tell him and he would get it. Or he'd hate me.

My mind swayed between that song and Rohan and Graham and how stupid I was all the time. Especially about him. I left him to keep my mom's mistakes from repeating in my life. But it wasn't my mom's history I should've been worried about repeating—it was my own. I was doing a fantastic job at fucking things up.

I reached out and placed my hand on Graham's arm. "I'm—" I started. I'm what? What am I?

Graham waited, June waited, I waited for my brain to function. There was nothing.

"I should go," he said, pointing to the bag in his hand. "Groceries. But get the peach ice cream. It's homemade and it's probably the best."

June smiled. "Noted."

Graham cleared his throat. "See you later, Cass."

"See ya," I said. He lingered there for a second, eyes on me, as if he was asking me to finish my sentence, and then he left. Wordlessly, June led us inside.

31.

Graham

SOMETHING WAS WRONG with Cassie. I
knew it because I knew her. I knew from the way she
bit the side of her lip, from the way she barely said
anything. Her eyes gave away everything. Whatever
was happening, it wasn't good.

I should've asked her. I should've made sure she
was okay, that she wasn't alone.

She had June; she wasn't alone.

But did June know her like I did?

They seemed close. Cassie didn't usually let people
get that close. She had a lot of practice at keeping
secrets.

She's fine, Graham. Get in the truck.

She was fine. It wasn't any of my business if she
wasn't. Three days of keeping my distance and they
had been good. I'd barely thought about her; of course
now that I've seen her again, it was going to take
three more to stop. I was doing this for me. I would be
leaving at the end of the summer. Two months. Two
months and I'd be in Texas and she'd be wherever and

our lives would finally, truly be separate.

We'd both move on. We'd both find our lives. I would stop wondering about her and remembering her touch and asking the what ifs. It was good I didn't ask because if I had, she would have told me and then we'd be that much closer. Closer for me and Cassie was trouble. Distance, now that was what I wanted.

I threw the grocery bag into the passenger seat, and backed out of the parking lot.

32.

Cassie

JUNE GAPED AT me while she ate her peach ice cream. She'd asked me to tell her about Graham and the whole story was too long, too complicated. The ice cream parlor was busy today. We were all crammed into the little space like sardines and this little kid next to us kept counting things.

"There's nothing to tell," I said. It was a bad lie, and I knew it as soon as it came out of my mouth.

"Bullshit. The other night was something with the way he bolted out of your place. That, out there, that was *way* more than 'nothing.' I already know he was the boy you were hung up when you came to Butler. Fill in the gaps."

I sighed, stirring the ice cream with my spoon. "He's been my best friend since I was eight."

"He was your first kiss?"

I nodded, taking a bite of the melting ice cream. It didn't settle well and it had nothing to do with the ice cream. I'll never forget the way he kissed me that first time over the fence between our backyards, after

160

I called him a jerk and he called me difficult and then we kissed. We were only fifteen but I knew that kiss changed me. It changed everything because it made everything that we'd both been ignoring become something. We were still ignoring something, bigger things, things that felt impossible to move past.

June leaned back. "First boyfriend?"

"Yeah," I said, pushing away the bowl. That kid still counted behind us, which was a good distraction from all the thoughts of Graham as my boyfriend. Holding my hand, walking me home, taking me on dates, sitting and doing absolutely nothing.

"First fuck?" She practically yelled it.

"June!" I screeched. The mother behind her gave us a dirty look, and June laughed.

"He was, okay." She pushed the spoon around in her bowl. "Is he good?"

I groaned. "That's not what we're talking about."

But my brain went there anyway. I was sixteen the first time Graham and I had sex. We hadn't been dating that long, but he'd already known everything about me, and it'd felt like we'd always been together. That weekend his parents were away; I went inside his house without knocking. He was in his room watching TV and when he saw me I remember him smiling. I curled up beside him, kissed him and said I knew he was the one; I was ready if he was. He spent most of our first time asking if I was all right, and we were both nervous and determined. It was awkward but perfect because we loved each other.

But then it got incredible when he figured out how to touch me. I remembered how he felt when I sunk my fingers into his shoulders and nibbled that place behind his ear that made him lose control. How it was when he'd move inside me and make my whole body fold at his touch.

"Oh my God, he is. You're blushing!" June yelled, slamming her hand on the table.

"Stop it," I whispered. My mind still flowed with thoughts of being with Graham, and I tried to block them out. I couldn't close my eyes because they'd be there more vividly, so I sighed.

June laughed and looked pleased. "I knew he had to be good. You can tell with some people," she said. She didn't look away from me when she took another spoonful of ice cream. "Really good?"

I groaned. "June, seriously."

She threw her hands up. "Okay. So he was your first rodeo—*only* rodeo aside from Rohan. So what happened? There's obviously still something between you."

She was wrong about that part. "There's nothing between us. We're just friends. Sort of."

"Sort of?"

"It's hard to go back to that after everything, but we're both trying."

"Outside didn't seem like trying. Well, it did: trying not to fuck each other right there on the sidewalk."

The mother gasped and grabbed her counting kid. I glared at June. "That's not how it is."

Was it? I thought about the look in his eye, and how hard he was trying not to notice I was upset. And the other night at my house, the way he stared at me like he was remembering or imagining. That couldn't mean anything. I'd done the same thing hundreds of times...but then I did want something. Graham had plenty of opportunities; she was reading too much into it.

She shook her head. "I promise you, it is. That boy still likes you, and you still like him."

"He's moved on, June. I had the chance and it's gone now. I've ruined his life enough."

"How so?"

"I left him to go to school." I stirred the ice cream some more. It was turning into a milkshake now.

"So?"

She seriously wanted me to spell it out. "So, it broke him. That's what I do. I break people."

"Fuck that!" she said. I looked at her again. I forgot how that was her favorite word. "Graham seems pretty solid to me. Get him back."

"I can't do that."

"Oh, I think you can, but get one thing clear, Cassie Harlen." She leaned into me. "You didn't break him. And if you did, then you broke yourself too. I remember when you were still in pieces, but you healed. He seems healed, too. That's what breaks do, they heal and then they grow back stronger."

I shook my head. "You don't know the whole story, June."

"So tell me."

"YOU'RE SERIOUSLY MESSED up," June said. She didn't even blink. It was the first thing she'd said in eighty-six seconds since I finished the story about Graham and how I left.

"Gee, thanks," I said.

"Seriously. That is the biggest bunch of shit I have ever heard, and I grew up in the system."

I stopped walking. "I was eighteen, and I was scared—"

She stopped, too. "And now you're nineteen—and

you did the same thing to Rohan. You decided you were out and you left. You were going to do it to me, too."

"But I didn't."

She threw her hands in the air. "Only because I caught you! Admit it, Cassie."

"Admit what?" I crossed my arms. I didn't like this conversation.

June lit a cigarette. She wasn't supposed to smoke in the park, but I didn't care enough to get into that fight. She took a drag and left me waiting. "You're too terrified that if anyone saw the real you, they would be fucked up for life because you are fucked up."

"I'm not fucked up!" I shouted. Some families walking around us all stared.

"The hell you aren't," she said. June started walking, cigarette in hand, and I moved with her. "We all are. We all have issues. Life sucks, but you can't act like the world owes you something because you got dealt a shitty hand. It seems like God or the Universe or Queen Shiva—whatever the hell you want to call it—gave you a smoking hot boy. Twice, I might add. One who has never given up on you, and you left him. I would be pissed if I was him."

"He is pissed," I said.

"What did he say when you told him why you left?"

I looked away and bit the side of my jaw. June grabbed my shoulders so I was forced to look at her. "Christ, you didn't tell him?"

"He's over me! He has a girlfriend and a plan and I stumbled back into his life. I can't be selfish again. I'm trying to do the right thing here and let him live his own life."

"Who are you trying to convince?"

"You."

June shook her head and crossed her arms. "I think

you mean yourself." June was a little scary right now. I'd never seen her this worked up. "One, you're not doing the right thing for him; you're doing the right thing for *you*. The right thing for Graham would be to apologize. Two, that boy is not over you. Girlfriend or not, no one looks at a girl that way who's 'just a friend.' He still has feelings for you."

I needed her to stop saying that. It was really annoying that she came in here like she knew everything. She didn't. "He doesn't."

June grabbed my arm when I tried to storm off ahead of her. "And you're an expert on feelings? God, Cassie. You haven't even talked to Rohan since you left him. He told me he called you."

She talked to Rohan about me? What was she trying to do? I already felt guilty enough for how I left that. I yanked my arm away and we walked on in silence. She was kind of right. I was fucked up. Who does the same thing to two people? The worst part was that I didn't see it.

"Listen," June said, "that was harsh."

"Don't apologize."

June scoffed. "I'm not. I meant every syllable," she said, tossing her cigarette into a trash. "You made some mistakes, but own up to them and fix it. It's not too late yet."

Where did I start? Just thinking about all of them was as if I was tornado who'd destroyed a whole town and left all the shit I'd broken. Where did I start with that? How did I fix it? Graham felt impossible to reach now, no matter what June thought about how he felt. Rohan was a mystery; I owed him something, but what and how to give it to him, I wasn't sure.

We crossed the street leaving the park. Neither of us had spoken for the whole five-minute walk back to the car. "You know why Stevie Nicks is a rock legend?"

"Enlighten me," I said.

"Because legends change the game," June said. She paused and took a breath. Her eyes wandered around the park like she was seeing it all for the first time, green and monkey bars and kids running around, then she continued. "Stevie Nicks put women on the map. She wrote her own music and she entered the industry at the right time. She set a bar, told the truth in her songs, and spoke to the soul. She didn't care what people thought and she was true to herself. That's the woman you are named after."

I watched June as we walked. Under what she put out there—the hair colors, the clothes, the attitude, the sex—she was something else entirely. I couldn't quite figure her out, but I thought that maybe I should start trying. That's what friends did—called each other out and saw beyond what they put in the world.

"Legends don't raise the bar; they set a new one," June said as I opened the car door. "Set the bar, Cassie."

33.

Graham

COOL AIR SEEPED through the open window while I filled out the paperwork for school and tried not to think about anything else. Cassie's laughter flooded my ears, carried to my room in the breeze. I froze and listened. Her laughter was met with Mrs. H's, and what had to be June's. I pushed back the curtain to see outside. The girls were in the backyard, light shining from bug repellent lamps. I wondered what they were talking about that made them all laugh so loudly.

I couldn't keep doing this. The sooner I was out of this town, away from Cassie, the better.

"What are we doing for dinner?" Molly asked, wrapping her arms around my neck.

I peered at her over my shoulder. Her long blonde hair was up out of her face, eyes on me. *You have this great girl; don't fuck it up, Tucker.*

"Whatever you want. We can go out."

She shrugged, moving her hands down my chest. "I was thinking we could stay in."

I raised my eyebrow and pressed my lips against her arm. "That's a good plan."

"Are you almost done?"

"Almost," I said. "You?"

She sighed and sat on the corner of my desk. "I need a break. I wrote myself into a corner with my paper," she said. She had to write some social justice studies paper. I wasn't sure how that went with being a nurse, but apparently it did. "Rawls was right: everyone should be seen as equals, but where you come from does influence your view of right and wrong. But the other side is right, too: nationality and birthplace can't be parts of justice. That's how we got into this mess in the first place."

"Which one do you agree with?"

Molly paced my floor and her blonde hair fell loose from the ponytail. She was cute when she was fired up and it brought out her Georgia twang more. "I don't know—and I can't argue and defend both sides. I like what Rawls was saying, but it justifies actions. This is social justice, so actions can't be justified or it's the same cycle over and over again."

"You don't think where you come from helps create who you are?"

"Of course I do. We will always go back to what we know," she said. Molly twisted a ring around her finger while she paced through my living room. "If someone grows up learning that it's okay to eat sugar when they are upset, they will always turn to it. Even if they've spent ten years not eating sugar—put it in front of them when they're upset, and they will eat it. Even knowing it's wrong—"

"Why is sugar wrong?"

She shrugged. "Maybe it's illegal."

I tried to keep myself from smiling. "Okay. Go on."

She did. "Even knowing it's wrong to eat that sugar, on one side I can't blame them because it's what they were taught to do. The other says that equality means one law is wrong for everyone, regardless of background."

"What does sugar have to do with social justice?" I asked.

She threw up her arms. "Seriously? That's all you have to say?"

I pulled her down to my lap so she was facing me. "It's summer. Take a break."

"I still have to turn it in, that's the purpose of an online class," she said.

"Later," I said, moving my lips to hers. "It's break time right now."

Molly pressed her body into mine, and her hands trailed down my chest and into the waistband of my jeans. My body groaned at her touch, and my mind wandered to Cassie briefly and wished it were her. Molly stepped away and pulled off her shirt and let her hair down. When our lips met again, I ran my fingers through her hair, like I used to do with Cassie's, and kissed Molly harder to push Cassie out of my head. I could forget her and her touch if I tried hard enough.

But Cassie's laughter echoed through my room, and I wondered what Molly would say about my conditioning. Maybe she was viewing it wrong— maybe people needed something familiar to cling to, and that's why they went back. Because the unknown was scarier than the bad thing they didn't want.

Maybe I was conditioned to Cassie the same way Molly's fake person had to eat illegal sugar. I didn't want to think about Cassie, to have my thoughts wander to her or to have her voice taunt my memory, but I couldn't let it do anything else.

34.

Cassie

"YOUR MOTHER TOLD me that you've had a friend visiting for a couple weeks now," Dr. Lambert said at our next appointment.

"June, yeah," I said.

"How has that been?" she asked.

"Interesting," I said. June was the most real person I'd met. She knew what she was, what she wanted, and she didn't care if you liked her or not. She always said what she thought, wanted or not. Especially since our talk. It was refreshing. "I love being around her, but I didn't know she was coming."

"Why did she come?"

"She said I disappeared."

Dr. Lambert smiled. "You tend to do that. Why change that with June?"

"I trust her. I didn't want to lose her friendship." And until I said it, I didn't realize how true that was. "I told her everything."

The pen scribbled on Dr. Lambert's page. "What did she say when you told her about your mom and

Graham?"

I chuckled a little. "I mean, she was understanding, but she said I was pretty fucked up. Her words."

"That's quite a friend."

"She said other things, too, that I hadn't thought about."

"Like what?"

I recounted some of our conversation. The parts about being selfish, about me needing to fix things while I had the chance, about me setting a new bar. It felt like a good way to move on and deep down, I did want to move on. Be stronger. Be brave. Do something to deserve all the good people I had around me.

Dr. Lambert nodded. "How are you going to fix it?"

"I should probably start with Rohan."

Dr. Lambert flipped through her notes, and I wondered what she kept written there. "Why should you start there? I don't know much about Rohan. You've barely mentioned his name."

I shifted on the couch. "I was dating him at school, and then I left him. The same way I left Graham. He wrote a song about me; it's like number five on the Billboard charts."

"A song?"

I scrolled through my music. I'd bought it so I could torture myself with how much I sucked. I let the song play and watched Dr. Lambert's face for a reaction. She was stoic, jotting down a few lines here and there while she listened. When it was over, she said: "How does that song make you feel?"

"Like shit." I paused for a breath and turned off my phone. "What do I say?"

"I can't tell you that. If you feel the way you do and you think June was right about your actions, then what do you think the solution is?"

"Make it better," I said. Somehow. Whatever that was. Apologize.

"The best way to do that is to lay it all out there. No turning back. No excuses. Say your piece, accept what he has to say, and move on."

"That sounds easier than it will be."

"You're right. It does." Dr. Lambert leaned forward in her seat. "But, Cassie, if you want to find your path, to set the bar like June said, then you have to let go of the past or you will never be free from it. Do you want to spend your whole life running?"

"No," I said. And I really meant that.

"I was going to wait, but I think this is a good time to bring it up." Dr. Lambert paused. "Joyce and I have been talking, and I'd like to do a group session with you and her and me."

"In one room?"

"I want you to tell your mother the things you've told me. I think she's ready. I think you're ready. You both need this."

"I don't know if I can."

"You can," she said. "And you should. Set the bar, Cassie."

"When?"

"Soon," she said.

I exhaled. "Okay."

Dr. Lambert smiled.

ROHAN'S SONG "GONE Gone Gone" played everywhere—and it was clear that I couldn't ignore this. I didn't want to be haunted by that song for the rest of my life. I sat cross-legged in my room, and dialed Rohan's number. My heart was in my throat while it rang. Twice, three, four times.

"Hey," he said breathlessly.

My words rushed out. "Hey, it's Cassie."

"This is Rohan. I'm not around my phone, so leave me a message—"

Someone screamed in the background, and another bandmate's voice popped on the line. "And check out our fucking song on iTunes, bitches!"

Rohan laughed. "What he said."

Voicemail. My stomach churned. It would've been easy to leave a message. If I said, "Hey, I'm sorry," and left it there. The automated voice told me to leave a message and I wanted to, but I couldn't do that. I had to face this myself. I'd left a note once and this time I needed to talk to him. I hung up as someone knocked on my door.

"Harlen?"

"Come in," I said, but June was already opening the door.

"What's going on?"

"I tried Rohan—no answer."

"You called him?" She was almost proud.

I nodded. "I need to fix it. Every time I hear that song I cringe. I need to apologize to him and to explain why I left."

June smiled and plopped onto my bed. "Then you're telling Graham?"

I shook my head. It was already early June. August wasn't that far, and with August came his independence. "I'm not telling Graham."

"I think you're making a mistake."

"I'm not," I snapped.

"I really wanted you two to make up before I left so

I could hear all the sexy details."

There weren't going to be sexy details. "Left? You're leaving?"

She nodded, and bit her fingernails. "Saturday."

Saturday? "But it's already Monday! You didn't tell me."

"It happened this morning," she said. She picked at the corner of her fingers, and she seemed nervous. June was never nervous.

"Where you going?" I asked.

She shook her head and curled her legs under her. "LA. My sister is there."

"Foster sister?"

June shrugged. "Real one."

"You have a sister?" I asked. She'd never mentioned a sister. I studied her face, looking for some clue about how she felt, but she kept her face motionless.

"We're not that close."

A sister. Why wouldn't she tell me about a sister? "So why leave then?"

"I have family shit too, Cassie."

"Right. Of course." I liked her being here. When she left, I'd be alone here with my mom. Not that it was the worst thing, but when she was here I could pretend I had something waiting for me. If she was gone then that was gone too.

June slapped my leg. "Are you getting clingy? I swear to God I will drop your ass, too, Harlen."

"Me? Clingy? Never!" I threw my arms around her and she laughed, but she didn't move away from my hug. She hugged me back.

"One thing we have to do before I leave: go to your miraculous beach."

"That we can do."

35.

Graham

I WAS WALKING to my truck, off to do another job that James needed some help with because extra money was always a good thing. I opened the front door to see June spread out in the backyard, in a bikini and an overgrown hat. She read a book with some shirtless guy on the cover.

"You know that the sun is bad for you, right?" I yelled, as I walked down the yard near her.

She spread her arms out. "Yeah, but a girl needs a tan, and the sun is free."

My eyes wandered past her toward the house, but it didn't look like anyone was in there. No music, no lights. "All alone today?" I asked.

She nodded and lowered her book to the ground. "Cassie and Joyce had an appointment. I'm relaxing before I go to LA."

"You're leaving?" I had a feeling that Cassie probably didn't like that idea. I didn't know June well, but she was good for Cassie. She needed more people to call her out on shit.

"Yup. Gotta go see my own family," she said. "We're

going to the beach tomorrow, if you're around."

The beach all day with Cassie in a bikini? I'd seen her in a bikini, and I wasn't that dumb. I knew there was no way I could do that. I was too weak. "Can't. Enjoy your sun though."

Cassie in a bikini was glued in my brain. She used to have this pink one with polka dots. I shook my head trying to force it away and took a few steps before June yelled my name. "She's different, you know." I turned back to her. "Cassie. She's not the same as she was when she left you."

Not the same? June didn't even know Cassie before she left. How could she judge that? She didn't know what went on in her head—hell, I didn't even know that half the time.

"You didn't really know her," I said back. I didn't need this; I was going to be late, but I was also curious. What did she think she knew?

June stood and moved closer to the fence between us. "I didn't know her then, but I know her now," June said, getting nearer to me. I could've left. I could've walked away because I didn't even know June in any way that mattered. I didn't have to listen, but my feet wouldn't move.

"I knew her right after. Met her the first week of school and she was this fragile little thing. I always knew she had something big, some kind of sadness that she was lost in." June was only inches from me. I could smell the coconut sunscreen. "I know because lost people—we can sense the confusion in other lost people."

"You're lost?" I asked. June didn't seem lost. She seemed sure of herself.

"I'm fucking Peter Pan."

I took a step away from her. "Well, thanks. I'll keep

that in mind if I need to never grow up."

"You're lost, too," she said a little louder. I turned back to her again. "I can see it."

What the fuck was up with this girl?

"I'm not lost. I know exactly where I'm going," I said. "To work."

June smiled as if I'd said the funniest thing ever. Crazy, that's what she was.

"There are different kinds of lost. Cassie lost her way, but I think you've lost something else completely. You just don't want to admit it."

I scoffed. "You don't really know me, June." Only I couldn't help but feel something tugging inside me. She was hitting a nerve. One that I didn't even know I had.

"I'm not trying to make you mad, I'm merely saying what I see," June said. She walked away from me back toward her spot. It was an out. I should've left it there, but I wanted to know what she thought she knew. Whatever it was, she was wrong.

"Which is what?" I yelled.

June faced me again, and took a step. "A guy who's trying really hard to ignore the fact that he's still in love with the girl next door."

"I'm not—" I clenched my fist. I wasn't in love with Cassie.

"A guy who's really scared right now, almost as much as that girl he's trying not to love."

June challenged me with a look in her eye. Her face was serious. She really believed this. She really thought I still loved Cassie. I wasn't scared. What the hell did I have to be scared of? Even more...

"What does Cassie have to be afraid of?" I asked. It was a little more aggressive than it should've been, but this wasn't cute anymore. She was digging up stuff that she didn't have any idea about. I didn't like it. "Leaving was her decision. I'm the one she hurt. I'm the one she left behind!"

"Have you ever asked her why she left?" June yelled. I paused. I hadn't. I still hadn't. I'd thought about it, but I couldn't bring myself to do it. June shook her head at me. "For someone who says he knows where he's going, you don't really seem to be looking for the answers."

"I don't need answers," I said. And I didn't need them. Cassie didn't want to get married; she didn't want me or to do any of the things we'd talked about. She'd left. She did all of it without talking to me. Those answers were pretty fucking clear.

June removed her sunglasses and looked me square in the eye. She seemed like she was going to say something, but then changed her mind. "My crack whore mom abandoned me when I was four years old for her drug dealer. My dad was never around. My sister left me for a foster family with lots of money and pretended I didn't exist for years. I never asked why—not why my mom left or why my dad left or why my sister left me to bounce in and out of shitty foster home after shitty foster home."

The words came out quick in one breath. June paused, glanced away from me, and then started again. "I never asked, but that didn't mean I didn't want answers. I did, but I was too scared to search for them, and of what they meant for me when I got them." She paused. "So fine, I don't know you that well, but I know how important answers are, and the source to all your answers lives twenty feet from where you're standing."

I did have an opportunity to find out something, and I was too scared to hear her tell me why I wasn't enough. I could pretend that Cassie and I were friends, that I didn't think about what we had before or what we could have again, but it was pretending. Friends didn't think about their friends the way I thought about Cassie. They didn't feel whatever it was I felt. I glanced back at June, trying to think of what to say to her story, but I didn't have anything. She was right though: I had to stop being scared.

June smiled and slipped her sunglasses back on.

"It was really great to meet you, Graham," she said. With that, she turned away from me, lowered herself back onto her towel, and shoved her earbuds in her ears.

36.

Cassie

THERE WAS NOTHING else I could say to my mom. I wasn't sure what other things were valid. For the last forty minutes, Dr. Lambert made me tell her story after story, to rehash all the things my mom and I had been through and how I'd felt about them all. Mom sat on the other side of the couch, a whole cushion between us. She wasn't permitted to respond until my story had ended, but she cried the whole time I spoke.

Dr. Lambert was in front of us, and in the distance between Mom and me, it felt a lot closer than normal. I wondered if this was how she was when it was just Mom. Her voice was softer today when she spoke. "Joyce, what's running through your head at this moment?"

Mom shifted on the couch; I didn't want to be near her, but I couldn't look away. I had this need to see that what I'd said had really been heard. I didn't know what good it would do, but it did feel better to have it all out there.

"I understand what you said before about how my denial of this problem has caused pain to those I love the most. To Cassie." She looked at me when she said my name.

"It's not a problem, Joyce."

Mom nodded her head. "Right. This disorder. A problem I can fix but the only way to 'fix' bipolar is to accept it and take actions to keep it under control."

Mom recited that as if she'd heard it all her life. A song that she loved and could hum without hearing. I watched her with Dr. Lambert, and it was familiar, open in a way that I never had with anyone. Not even with Graham.

"I want to take my life back," Mom said. I stared at her. Mom had this freedom now, all because I said what I said. How was it possible that I had that much power over her emotions?

Dr. Lambert turned her attention to me. "Cassie, what are you thinking at this moment?"

"I don't know."

"Yes, you do," she said. I closed my eyes. "This is a time to be honest."

"I'm jealous." I hadn't meant to say that, and as soon as the words were out, I regretted them. The looks on their faces, the shock at my answer, pierced me. I hadn't known I was jealous.

"You should probably clarify," Dr. Lambert said.

I waved them off. This was stupid. "Never mind. Forget it."

"Cassie—"

"Mom gets to come here and I get to unload all my shit on her, so she can decide to change her life. It's awesome, really. It seems so easy after everything. I love her." I looked at Mom. "I love you. I do."

"I sense a 'but," Mom said.

I crossed my arms. "But life isn't that easy. We make a mistake and we have to work our asses off to fix it."

"It's still going to be hard. I promise you this is only the beginning for Joyce, Cassie," Dr. Lambert said. I didn't want that promise. Beginnings were hard. Endings were hard. Everything was fucking hard.

"I know. I know it's going to be hard, and I will be here, just like I've always been," I said.

Dr. Lambert placed her hands in her lap. "Then, why are you jealous?"

I looked at Mom instead. "What do you want, Mom? More than anything—what do you want?"

She bit her lip. She seemed hesitant, but then she said, "Forgiveness. Understanding. A chance to move past this and to live again."

"Exactly." I stood and paced around the room. I wasn't supposed to stand, but I didn't care what I was supposed to do that day. "You know what you want and you get it. I don't."

"You don't get what you want?" Dr. Lambert asked. Mom watched us go back and forth like a Ping-Pong ball.

"I don't," I said. "I don't even know what I want beyond the thing I can't have anymore." I picked up a slinky off the table and moved it through my hands. "That's the part about all this that sucks, because I can tell you all the shit that went down my whole life. The things you missed, the messes you made because you were sick—but the one thing that your bipolar condition caused that I can't fix is the one thing I can't blame on you. Because I did it all on my own."

Mom paused and inhaled. "Graham."

I stopped a few inches from my side of the couch. "I was going to marry him, Mom. I never told you that."

"I know," she said.

I never told her that. I didn't get to. "You know?"

She nodded, scratching her neck quickly and twisting to see me. "He came by the night you left asking for you. That's when he found out about school, and I found out about your proposal."

"You never mentioned it," I said, lowering myself to sit on the back of the couch.

"Neither did you."

I stared at Mom. Of course Graham told her—they'd been here together without me. I just assumed, I guess, that since he never told his parents he'd never told mine. I bet he was pissed when she didn't know. That was the one thing I was supposed to do on my own. It was the whole reason I went over there.

Dr. Lambert cleared her throat. "Cassie, perhaps you should back up. Tell your mom what happened."

I moved to the window. I knew I should've sat down, but I couldn't bring myself to do it. "Why did you always tell me that dad died?" I blurted.

"Richard?"

I nodded and turned, leaning against the window. "You spent my life telling me he died. I went over that night to tell you Graham proposed to me, and you were in a state. Your room was a mess, and you were lost in your own memories. You thought I was someone else, and you told me dad left you because he couldn't handle you. Couldn't handle it."

Mom shook her head and looked away from me toward the floor. "I don't really want to talk about Richard, Cassie."

Dr. Lambert touched Mom's shoulder. "But Cassie does, Joyce. You should tell your daughter the truth. It seems like she needs it."

"I don't think I can," Mom whispered.

The room was quiet, save the ticking of the clock

counting down the time left in our session. I count them as they pass. What was so bad that Mom couldn't tell me? Did I really want to know the truth? Yes. Yes, I did. I needed to understand how she lied. How she kept something so important from me all my life. I kept moving around the room, unable to calm myself enough to sit.

Fifteen minutes later, Mom spoke up.

"It was 1977," she said. Her voice was low, but it seemed like a scream in the silent room. "I was twenty, brand new to the music industry, and I had this little nothing-now band who were the openers for Fleetwood Mac. Richard was their roadie."

I knew that part. That they'd met at a Fleetwood Mac concert. Mom spoke louder as the story continued. "He was such an ass, called me 'little girl' and had this cocky smile. The whole time before the show we fought; that's all we'd done for days, but we were arguing about something when Stevie came on and started singing "Angel." I don't even remember the fight anymore—something silly I guess—but then he said, 'You are the most infuriating woman in the world,' then he kissed me."

I've never heard that whole story. I lowered myself into my spot on the couch, and Mom was smiling. It was barely there, but it was a smile.

"It was a whirlwind for us, Cassie," she said. "I changed my whole life for him. It's how I got so involved with the band. It's why your name is what it is. They united us—their music. It was hard, but we made it work. He toured with them and I went along my own path. Eight years we did that, until we were married in 1985. We bought the house here, a neutral place away from everything, and we carried on."

I could tell that she was remembering from her

slight smile, a furrowed brow. I'd seen it enough times to know.

"Things were never great with us after we married," she said. Her voice changed, her shoulders dropped and she averted her gaze. "Travel's hard on a marriage. We would go months without seeing each other—me with my bands, him with whatever gig he could find. I ended up pregnant, and we weren't trying. We'd never even talked about kids, not with our lives, but there you were." She smiled at me, but I could see a little sadness in her eyes. "I decided to take a break until you were a few months old, so I passed on my bands to some co-workers and moved into our house. You have his eyes, you know."

I knew. I'd seen pictures. Mom's chestnut hair and Dad's cobalt eyes. I got the best of both of them.

Mom looked from Dr. Lambert to me and back again at Dr. Lambert. "He was never there. And when he was there, we fought. A lot. I had post-partum— that's when it all started and we didn't know—but he didn't understand. I couldn't take care of you like I needed and one day, when you were two, he said he was leaving. That was the last time I ever heard from him, except for the divorce papers."

I let out a breath. "Why wouldn't you tell me?"

She reached for my hand. I gave it to her. "I didn't want you to think it was you. Richard was a good man, Cassie, but we lived a hard life. He had a passion. I had a passion. You know how you feel about Graham? I don't think he ever felt that for me, nor I for him. That was music for us."

"And you gave it up for me," I said.

Mom squeezed my hand. "It was the best decision for you. I love you. You needed a mother. I'm sorry I failed at it."

"You didn't fail."

"I did," she said with a smile. "But I tried."

"It's not your fault."

"It isn't yours either," she said.

I scooted closer to her. "You told me that night he left because he couldn't handle your episodes."

She sighed. "I have no doubt that influenced his decision. It's hard to watch the person you love be lost. You've experienced that; not everyone is as strong as you. But Richard had a void that only music could fill. I knew that from the beginning, but I thought I would be enough like he was for me. Or like I told myself he was for me."

"That's why I left Graham."

Mom touched my face. "Why?"

I felt myself breaking around her. "Because I didn't want him to be stuck with me in case I was like you. I didn't think he could handle it."

"Graham? Oh, honey. That boy can handle anything," Mom said.

"I didn't want him to have to handle me. That's not a relationship."

Neither of us said anything, but I felt connected to my mom for the first time as we sat there and she stroked my hand. More than I ever had.

"Cassie, I think there's another reason that you don't even want to admit to yourself. Something holding you back, and it's not that you're not sick, Cassie," Dr. Lambert said. I shook my head. There was no other reason. "You said you were jealous that your mom knew what she wanted and that she could get it now. What do you want?"

"I don't know."

"Yes, you do," Dr. Lambert said, nodding toward me.

Right. I'd said that before, too.

"To not be like you," I said to Mom. I expected her to be upset, but she wasn't. Instead, she patted my hand with hers.

"What, specifically?" Dr. Lambert asked.

"Alone."

"Why do you think you're alone?"

I paused. It was harder to say it than I could admit. The words were stuck in my throat. "Because you were right and June was right—I kept everyone out. I pushed them all away to protect them, but really I was protecting myself."

"From what?" Dr. Lambert asked.

"From everything," I admitted.

Mom hugged me, and for the first time in all my life, I felt like she was my mom. Mom, instead of the person I was taking care of. Like it was for me, and not for her or for show, and tears welled up in my eyes. I tried to contain it, but I wanted to sob and never stop.

"Oh, Cassie," she whispered in my ear. "Your father had a mantra that he said every morning, 'You can't live your life in fear of what could be—if you do you'll never live it.'"

"Dad used to say that?"

She nodded. "Every day."

Graham told me that, too. Maybe it was a famous quote or something.

38.

Graham

MOLLY SIGHED NEXT to me and ran her fingers down my back as I rolled off her. She pressed her lips against my neck, and laughed lightly. "What's gotten into you tonight?"

I smiled. "It's been a while since I've seen you."

"That's not entirely my fault," she said.

I didn't miss the tone in her voice. I'd been avoiding her for the last few days. There was a lot going on, and I wasn't sure exactly what I was supposed to do with my Cassie feelings, especially after June confronted me. I hadn't stopped thinking about it. Not that I could tell Molly any of that. No sense in stirring up trouble. I kissed Molly's shoulder, and she squealed and pulled me into her, pressing her mouth against mine.

Her hands ran through my hair as I kissed her. When we needed to stop for breath, she muttered something about going to sleep. Sleep would be good. Her hand fell away from me, and I turned onto my side. A contented hum filled the room, and she grew still next to me. I was drifting off to sleep, but June's voice played in my head.

"*A guy who's trying really hard to ignore the fact that he's obviously in love with his old fiancée. A guy who's really scared right now, almost as much as that girl he's trying not to love. Have you ever asked her why she left?*"

Why hadn't I asked Cass about leaving? I should do that. If June was right, I should find out. Maybe tomorrow. I couldn't wait any longer. She was right there, and I'd been waiting almost a year. Maybe there was a reason. I needed to find it. To not be a pussy. I'd ask her and then I could put it all behind me. Cass and me could be a memory, finally.

"Night," she muttered.

"Night, Cass," I said.

This is nice. Silent and calm and warm. My eyes started to drift and she shifted on the bed and inhaled sharply. I turned around to see what was wrong, and she was sitting up, frowning.

"What did you say?" she asked.

"What?"

"You called me 'Cass'?" Her voice was high and she tightened the sheets up around her chest.

I scrambled up. "No, no I didn't do that."

She scoffed, jumping off the bed. "Yes, you did."

I didn't say her name. Why would I say her name? I tried to think to three seconds ago. In my silence, Molly rushed around the room, grabbing her clothes. I jumped out of the bed, too.

"Molly, I wasn't even thinking about her. I'm tired, that's all," I said. Which was obviously a lie. *Shit.* She slid on her jeans, and glared at me. "I didn't mean anything. I didn't even realize I said that."

She put her shirt over her head. "That's the problem, isn't it? You haven't been the same since she returned. I should've known."

"Molly," I begged.

She shook her head. "I'm going home."

The door slammed behind her.

39.

Cassie

JUNE WAS SPRAWLED out across the backseat of the car with her head on one side and her feet on the other. Mom was next to me, smiling and singing along to the playlist that she helped me create. I even put a few tracks from some of June's music—bands I'd never heard of because I was, indeed, a music snob. I was missing out on something good because I hadn't tried to find it.

"This is my jam, Cassie—turn it up!" June yelled from the backseat.

"Who's this again?" I asked as the music started up. It wasn't a bad intro.

"The Lone Bellow. They are going to be big, girl. Mark my words."

Music mingled in the wind as we sped across the interstate toward the beach. June sang off-key, and Mom smiled the whole time. Enjoyed the moment.

I kept looking over at her as we drove, waiting for something to change. For her smile to slip or her eyes to look at me and not see me, but that didn't happen for the whole drive. It wasn't much time, but I'd take it.

This wasn't a pretty day. It was just a day.

A summer day at the beach with my mom and my best friend. It was almost like I was normal.

40.

Graham

I SAT INSIDE my apartment and stared at my phone. Molly would call me back. She had to call me back so we could talk. I'd left her three messages since last night, but I wanted to explain. I wasn't sure what I would say. I'd made a mess of things, but I didn't want her to hate me.

I dialed her number again. If she didn't answer this time I'd go to her work. I'd stop by her aunt's house. Something.

Three rings, and she picked up.

"What do you want?" Her voice was sharp. She was angry. She had every right to be.

"Please let me explain, Molly."

"I don't want your excuses. Please stop calling me."

"Ten minutes, Molly. Please give me ten minutes. I don't want to do this on the phone."

She was quiet, and I wasn't sure what she was thinking. Then: "I get off at eleven."

I exhaled into the phone. "Thank you, Molly. Thank you."

"Don't thank me. Ten minutes—that's all you get."
Then, she hung up.

41.

Cassie

JUNE SPENT MOST of her time in the water, while Mom slept on the beach. June had never been to the Atlantic, and this was different water. That's what she kept saying; whether different was better or worse she never said. While she was in the ocean, I was sprawled out on the sand. I couldn't stop listening to these new bands—in the four hours we'd been there, I'd listened to three albums completely through and took some notes in my notebook. There were a couple songs I loved, a couple that I thought I could've been arranged differently to bring out some of the uniqueness, and only one or two that fell short. Overall, it was good, and it was from this century.

June plopped down next to me and snatched an earbud from my ear. I smiled, and when a few lyrics passed June sat up on her knees. "Is Cassie Harlen listening to my music? The world is ending!"

"It's good."

She threw her arms over her head. "The sky is going to fall!"

I pushed her and she laughed. "Seriously."

"Have you tried Rohan again?"

"Whoa, hello one-eighty," I said, pausing the song so I wouldn't miss anything.

"New music, old musician boyfriend—it totally transitions."

I shrugged. Rohan was still in the "unfinished" column. "I've called him twice. I left a message last time."

"Third time's a charm, right?" June said.

"You're pushy."

"That's what good friends are for!"

June lay on her back, dripping some water from her hair onto my journal. I moved it before she completely ruined it.

"I thought good friends were for support and encouragement?"

"They are. How do you think they do that?" June definitely had the pushy down.

We didn't move while the sound of the waves and kids nearby and my mom snoring filled the air. It was busy enough to feel alone and lost in the noise. Everyone scattering in his or her own path and not looking back. Even the wind had a direction, and I was stuck.

Stuck unmoving // Destiny looming

I closed the journal.

"So what's up with your sister?" I asked, looking at June. She adjusted her sunglasses, and let out a sigh. "How long are you going?"

"I don't know. Until school maybe? I haven't thought about it."

I couldn't see her face well, but her tone changed. There was something about LA and her sister that she didn't want to talk about. I started to ask when Mom popped up next to us abruptly.

"We should go," Mom said, stretching. "I want to make a stop."

⌒⟁⟁

THE OLD STRIP of pink, blue and orange stores used to sit on the right side of the highway off exit sixty-seven, that's why we would always go before home. The stores were no longer colored—no longer this magical place over the rainbow. They were an industrial shade of metal. Mom frowned and deep lines appeared on her forehead.

"What's this place?" June asked.

Nothing anymore.

"Cassie and I used to come here when she was a kid," Mom said.

"It was better then," I added.

"What is it?" June asked.

I unbuckled my seatbelt, but Mom grabbed my arm and shook her head. "A memory that I'd like to keep as it was," she said. I looked back at the building. Mom was right. Even if this place only mattered because it was Pretty Day, it still mattered. It was as deeply a part of me and us as the bad ones.

Some things were better off left in the past where they couldn't be touched or changed. Others were full of promise.

"We should go," she said.

I couldn't agree more. I put on another one of June's albums, and we left.

42.

Graham

I WAS ALREADY at the door when Molly came to it. Her blonde hair was curled, and I always liked that. She looked less than happy to see me. I had some major damage to repair here, if I could even do that. Molly crossed her arms over her chest as she approached me.

"Hey," I said. I opened the door a crack to let her come in. She hesitated at first, but then she went past me up the stairs.

Molly was in my living room, unmoving, while we stared at each other. I tried to hug her, but she took a step back from me. "I don't really know why I'm here," she said.

I reached out for her hand, but she wouldn't let me touch her. She even took another step back. I really messed this up. "I'm sorry. I'm so sorry. You have to know I didn't mean it."

"I don't know that," she said. She crossed her arms over her chest. "You've been different since she came back."

"There's nothing between her and me."

"You called me her name last night!" Molly yelled. Her eyes were glassy and I really didn't want her to cry. "What do I do with that?"

I shoved my hands into my pockets.

She shook her head. "What is it about her? You need to tell me. I deserve to know."

I didn't want to tell her. What could I say? She was Cassie. We had a history, an unfinished history, a relationship with no answers, an appeal and connection I couldn't explain. She wouldn't like any of that. How could I tell Molly what Cassie and I had been and not lose her? She shook her head and walked toward the door.

"Wait—" I yelled. She turned around to me. "She was the first girl I loved. I met her when I was nine." Molly's eyes widened, like she waiting for more. "This will take longer than ten minutes."

She sat on the couch across from me and I told her the whole story. All the details I'd never shared before. That Cassie and I had such a long history. That I held her up and let her guide me and planned to spend my life with her. That she left me and even after I went to get her back, she refused me.

When the story was done, Molly was quiet.

"Do you still love her?" she asked.

I didn't know how to answer. "I don't know."

"That's probably the first honest thing you've said in months."

Was it? I really meant what I'd said. I never meant to lie to her. I wasn't with Cassie, but I did wonder. I wondered a lot of things—why she left, what I meant to her, what she wanted, what I wanted. Was all that because I still loved her?

Molly stood up without another word. I jumped up

too.

"Don't leave," I said.

"I need to figure this out," she said, putting her palm up at me. She moved toward the door and I didn't stop her. I knew I didn't have the right to ask her to stay. Not when I didn't know what I wanted, or when I did know what I wanted and it wasn't something I'd sworn I was over. Either way, she left.

43.

Cassie

I STOOD OUTSIDE on the porch, and Mom and June were inside talking more about June Carter Cash. It seemed like the perfect time to step away. I inhaled and stared at Rohan's name and picture before I pushed the call button. I needed to start fixing things, and this one seemed a little easier than the one a yard away.

The phone rang, and rang and rang. I was nervous about what to say to him. He answered with: "I can't believe you're calling me."

"Yeah, I know it's random. I just—"

"I left you messages," Rohan said. A few of them. All deleted.

"I didn't know what to say," I said. That part was true. Even now, I was a little too nauseous to let my guard down, and I was the one who'd left. Silence echoed on the other end. I could hear him breathe, slightly, and the noise around him. Other voices, clattering.

"I'm sorry," I said. "I shouldn't have left like that. I

was wrong."

"I thought you were happy," he said. His voice was extremely calm. A lot calmer than I'd expected.

"I don't think I'd been happy for a year. I loved someone else. Someone who I hurt, and I tried to replace him with you. I'm sorry; that wasn't fair. I was too scared to leave, to admit what I'd done, and then my mom happened," I said. It was nice, actually, to say all that out loud. I hadn't admitted to anyone, barely even to myself, but this was freeing. "I freaked out, Rohan."

Rohan was quiet again except the noise around him. I expected him to yell, to say something, to call me a name, but he didn't. He let out this sort of short, stifled laugh. "You know what, Cassie? I think it was the best thing that's ever happened."

Okay, I did not expect that.

"Don't get me wrong, I was pissed. So pissed. You didn't answer and June said you called her once and I felt like I never mattered, but you made me."

"Made you?"

"The song I wrote about you? I'm doing what I love because of you. You left and I was thinking, 'What the hell am I doing? I don't want to be an engineer.' You leaving pushed me into music. You helped me in a weird, messed-up kind of way."

I smiled. "I take it back then."

"What?" he asked.

"I'm not sorry."

Rohan chuckled, and then he grew silent. "Take care, Cassie."

"You too, Rohan."

"I hope you find your happiness."

Then he hung up, and that was it. There was no yelling. No anger. We were extinguished, properly. I could let it all go.

I turned to go inside when I saw Molly headed back from Graham's place. She looked exhausted. I glanced back at my phone, but I knew she saw me watching her and she beelined toward the porch and me.

"Cassie," she called. This wasn't good.

"Molly," I said back.

"Can we talk?" she asked. Yeah, because that was what I'd wanted to do. Talk to Graham's girlfriend. I pointed to the chairs and she took a seat. "I don't really want to beat around the bush here. You still have feelings for him, don't you?"

I swallowed. "Graham and I have a histo—"

"That's not what I mean," she said. She looked as uncomfortable as I felt. "I know about him fixing things at your house, and bowling, and coming over to hang out with you. I don't really like games. Life is too short for that. So can we be honest with each other for a minute?"

I nodded.

"I like Michael—Graham, whatever you call him. Really like him. We've been together for seven months now, and when I met him, he was a mess," she said with a pause and I tried not imagine Graham as a mess. Or how leaving me at school changed him. That had been hard for me. I'd barely survived giving back his ring, and it was my choice. I couldn't imagine what it'd done to him...

"He was angry and confused. He didn't know which way was up. He told me once that he was broken by some girl he loved, and that was you. I was there when he put himself back together," Molly said. "But I'm not you, and you're back. He doesn't look at me the way he looks at you. I didn't want to admit it, but now—"

"There's nothing between us." I said. I did it with

a straight face, and if I didn't know myself, I would've believed it. We were nothing, but we were everything.

"Don't tell me that. He didn't spend weeks fixing my house. He didn't take care of my family when I left for college. He didn't save my mom from a burning building."

"He what?" I asked. We stared at each other for a second, and Graham's voice played in my ear. The one from that first call when he said Mrs. Pearson saved her, and firemen and the hospital. How he was there. He'd always been there.

"You didn't know?"

I shook my head. Graham saved my mom. He...?

Of course, Graham saved my mom.

Molly exhaled. "I'm not saying I want to give him up, because I like him. But I think you confuse him. Ever since you came back, he's been different. So please, let him go."

"What?"

"Let him go," she said, and then she left me and walked to her car.

I stared after her, squeezing my phone in my hand until she was out of sight. My knuckles started to ache. I wasn't anything to Graham. Was I? There had been some things before. No. It didn't matter.

Let him go.

What the hell? Was that what Graham wanted? That he wanted me to let him go? Fuck that. If he wanted that he could tell me himself.

44.

Graham

I COULDN'T SLEEP, again. I couldn't remember the last time I slept all night, but this time for a different reason. How did I feel about Cass? What was Molly going to do? I had to roam. I didn't know where I was going to go just after dawn, but when I opened my door, Cass was standing there. It was too early for this. Or late. This day sucked.

"You leaving?" she asked.

I shrugged. "Nowhere important."

"We need to talk."

The dreaded words. Great.

I opened the screen door for her and we went upstairs. I barely closed the living room door when she turned to me. She looked a little angry, but I hadn't done anything. I hadn't even spoken to her since the ice cream parlor.

"Your girlfriend came to see me earlier," she said. She picked up this little glass ball thing from the table and put it back down. Molly went to see her? That wasn't good. I watched her walk around my apartment.

"She told me that I needed to let you go."

"What?"

Cass flipped around to me. Her blue eyes were bright and wild. "Is that what you want?"

"Since when did what I want matter to you?" I asked. Cass never cared about what I had to say or think. If she had then we wouldn't be how we were right now.

"It's always mattered to me," she said.

I laughed. "It's never mattered."

Cass pushed me and I stumbled. She had a fire burning in her eyes. One that I hadn't seen since she got back. "What the hell, Graham? I thought we were going to be friends. You agreed to that. If you want me to let you go just say the word!"

I turned away from her. "I can't talk about this right now."

"Don't walk away."

"I'm not the one who walks away! That's you, Cass!" I yelled. I didn't like yelling, but she was so infuriating. She looked at me as if I'd slapped her. "Oh, sorry. I don't mean walk—I mean run away in the middle of the fucking night."

"You don't know what that was like for me," she said. Her voice was soft, and if I wasn't so pissed and tired, I would've cared.

She was right: I didn't know. That was because of her. "You're right—because you disappeared and wouldn't tell me a damn thing. God, you're so selfish."

"I'm selfish?" she squealed.

"Yes! You only think about yourself. About what you want and to hell with the rest of us."

Cass crossed her arms. "What about you? You made decisions and never even stopped to think about what I wanted!"

"I never had to think. You never had a problem telling me what you wanted before. You never had a problem pretending you wanted the same thing!" I had to get control. I'd never told Cass how I felt about all this, but it was sort of nice not holding the shit back anymore. I didn't care if I hurt her feelings. Not when she'd burned all mine without an apology or an explanation.

Cass took a step closer to me. "That's why you proposed to me when you knew I was trying to figure out the future."

"Our future. *Ours.* I thought it was ours. I stayed here for you. I did everything for you, so excuse me if I thought proposing to the woman I loved was the best solution for *our* future. You're the one who said yes— no one held a gun to your head!"

"You're just as selfish as me, Graham!"

I shook my head. "You're right. Silly me. I must not know what selfish means, because I thought it was you who left, not me. You who moved across the country and abandoned her mother. That's selfish, Cassie. And that was you, not me."

"Don't," she said. "That's not fair."

"Fair? You know what's not fair? I drove all the way to fucking Indiana to get you back. To ask you why you left, and you gave me back that ring without a second thought. You told me nothing. *That's* selfish."

Cass shook her head; her eyes watered and she took a step back. "Stop it."

I didn't stop. I couldn't once I'd started. Not after a year of not saying anything to her about it. "I've done everything for you. I'm selfish? Fine, I'm selfish because I waited for you—"

"I never asked you to—"

"—And I proposed to the girl I loved because

nothing made me as happy as when she smiled or when she said my name. Because there was no one who would ever compare to her in my head and she had this sad amazing little life, but she never let it stop her. She kept dreaming and that inspired me. And a woman like that? Yes, I had to spend my life with her."

She didn't say anything, but I had her attention. Good. I stepped closer to her. So close I could hear her breathing. I could feel it, and see her chest rise and fall. I could see the green in her eyes, and the way they looked glassy.

"If that makes me selfish, then yes, Cass. Yes, I'm as selfish as they come. I won't apologize for that."

45.

Cassie

GRAHAM TUCKER STOOD in front of me and gave this speech and somewhere in the middle, I knew he still felt that way. I did, too.

"If that makes me selfish, then yes, Cass. Yes, I'm as selfish as they come. I won't apologize for that."

I hurled myself into his arms, filling the inch that separated us, and pressed my lips against his. Graham seemed surprised at first, frozen, and it took him a moment to respond. Like his body was remembering me, but mine had never forgotten. I'd never let it. I'd never wanted to.

I pressed against him, feeling reckless and out of control. Then, he was ready. I felt the shift as his fingers dug into my hips and he pressed himself against me, his erection hard. Heat flowed between us, and his lips were hungry. He pushed me backward against the wall until there was no space between us and deepened the kiss. My hand trailed under the waist of his jeans. He moaned into my mouth, and his slightly calloused hands were all over my body. Rough when they trailed across my stomach as he kissed my neck, and my whole body exploded.

In this moment, there was no past or future. No trespasses, no arguments, and nothing to forgive. There was me and him and this. This was what I'd been missing. Graham and I had this electricity, this instant heat. He felt it, too. Whatever else we felt or knew, there was nothing like this. He brought me in closer to him. My hand tugged at the waist of his jeans, because I wanted him, and he wanted me, and we'd waited long enough.

46.

Graham

I WAS KISSING Cassie and it was everything I remembered it being. More, even. It was like no way we'd kissed before, and no way we'd kiss again. I wanted her. I focused on that part of myself, the part that wanted this more than air. That wanted her skin on mine, and her breath in my ear.

We stumbled backward toward the bed, never parting even to breathe. I pinned her against the wall, and her fingers trailed up my shirt. Each touch was an electric shock. I was with Cass. This was what I wanted, really wanted, but something lingered at the back of my mind. I tried to shut it out. I tried to keep kissing her and focus on her hands and her body...I couldn't ignore the call in my head that this was wrong. I could let it happen, but it shouldn't be this way. We had all these unspoken feelings and secrets between us. All this uncertainty. I had a girlfriend.

Cass pulled at my pants, and my body responded under her touch. I groaned at the pressure, but then I jumped away from Cass because she was fire and wind and lightning. She looked at me, face red and confused.

We were both panting. I was confused, too. I'd been nothing but confused since I called her after that fire. She was here, disheveled and beautiful and I—*God, what a mess*—I was the dumbest man alive for what I was about to say.

"We can't," I said. Even saying it hurt, because lies always hurt the most. We could've, but we shouldn't.

"Graham."

I had to look away. I couldn't say this and see her. Not when she was looking like that and we were about to have sex and everything inside me still wanted her. "I have a girlfriend, Cassie. I can't do this."

We didn't say anything for a long time. I tried to focus on a normal thought. All of my thoughts were Cassie. Her hands, her lips, her voice, her hips, the soft skin on her upper thigh, her—

"I didn't come over here to—"

"I know," I said. "This was a lapse, a wrong one."

She looked away from me. "I should go."

"Probably best for now," I said. I had to get her out of this room before my mind lost this battle to my body.

She slid on her shoes—I hadn't even realized she'd taken them off—and walked back toward the door. When she was almost there, she returned to me and stood right under me until I was forced to meet her gaze. Man, I loved those eyes.

"This wasn't wrong, Graham."

"I have to figure it out," I said. That part wasn't a lie. I didn't know what was right here, what was worth it.

"I know. I get it. But whatever you think about, this wasn't wrong. This was us, and we are never wrong."

I didn't respond, and Cass left me standing in the living room. I had to talk to Molly. I had a girlfriend, but I knew without a doubt that she wasn't the one I wanted. I've never felt that way for Molly, even if I tried. And I had tried.

I loved Cassie Harlen. I had never really stopped.

47.

Cassie

IT TOOK ME the rest of the morning to fall asleep, because all I could think about was Graham's lips on mine, his fingers sliding across my skin, the feel of him pressed against me. It was better than I remembered; I hadn't wanted it to end. I didn't go over there to kiss him. I made a mess of this. He called us wrong. He must hate me.

"Harlen?" June called, knocking on the door. I groaned in response. "At least you're alive. I'm coming in."

Her eyebrows furrowed when she saw me. "What happened?"

I looked her over. June had on her shoes, a jean jacket, and a purse. "You're leaving today!"

"Today's the day. Taxi should be here any minute."

"I can take you," I said, throwing off the covers. I was so busy moping that I almost missed her leaving.

"Nah, don't worry. The bus doesn't wait for goodbyes." She smiled, but I could see that she didn't want to leave either.

She sat next to me. I really didn't want her to leave. She was starting to make all the other shit make sense. Neither of us said anything at first.

"You're taking a bus all the way to California?" I asked.

June replied quickly, the words out in a rush. "Nah, back to school so I can grab things. Then, I'll fly to my sister."

I wanted her to stay. No getting clingy. When did she become so important to me?

"Why haven't you told me about your sister?" I said.

June smiled back at me. "I didn't know your mom was bipolar. Or that you had a fiancé." Whatever it was, she wasn't talking, but she'd talk when she was ready.

"Touché," I said. She was trying to be funny, but I could tell she was as hurt that I hadn't thought she was important enough to know the truth. Hopefully she knew it wasn't her, that it was me. Because I didn't want to face it.

"Now you know about her. There are just some things in my past that are complicated."

"I get it," I said.

She put her hand on my mine. "What happened last night?"

Everything happened. "I called Rohan, that was good. Molly came over."

"Uh-oh."

That didn't even begin to explain it.

What did I do now?

June stared at me, obviously wanting details. Maybe talking about it would be good. Would help it make sense. "She told me to let him go. How does she have the right to say that to me? So, I went over to Graham's and told him what happened. We fought, and then somehow, we kissed."

"You kissed?"

I shifted on the bed, and felt my body warm at the memory. "Made out."

Her eyes were wide, and she smiled a little. "Made out?"

Tears burned behind my eyes. Mostly because I was embarrassed, but even more because he did the right thing. I shouldn't have gone over there. I shouldn't have kissed him. What did I expect to happen?

"He stopped it," I said. That was the worst part. That he said it was wrong. We were never wrong, no matter what the circumstances. We were "Cass and Graham," and it was as natural as breathing.

"He did?"

I threw a pillow at her. "Stop repeating everything I'm saying! It's annoying."

June threw the pillow back at me. "So, you guys made out, and now what?"

That was the million-dollar question. I didn't know the answer. I didn't know if I wanted the answer. There were only two ways for this to end, and neither of them were good because in my head, they both ended in us not being together. "Now, he still has a girlfriend."

June gave me a thumbs-down. "How did you end things?"

"He said it was a mistake. I said it wasn't. I'm here. Now I don't know. I wait?"

"Yes, wait."

I started pacing. What was I waiting for? "I hate waiting."

"You know what you can do while you wait?"

I raised my eyebrows.

"Research."

"For what?" I asked, confused. How to ruin a life?

How to heal a broken heart? How to not kiss your ex-fiancé even though you want to? Too late on all those.

June shook her head in a "poor Cassie" sort of way. "You still need to pick a major, or a path, or whatever the shrink suggested."

I deflated. "Right." That wasn't the answer I wanted either. Fill the questions in with more questions.

A horn honked from outside, and suddenly I didn't want to say goodbye. I pulled her into a hug. "You'll call when you get there?"

"Of course. You'll call when you and Graham figure it out? I'll want all the details."

"If there are details."

"There will be." She winked. I wished I shared her certainty.

I walked her down the stairs and Mom hugged her, too. "You can come here anytime, June."

"Thanks, Mrs. Harlen. See ya," she said over her shoulder.

Mom and I watched from the doorway as June got into her cab, and then, when it drove off, it was the silence and us. This one was more normal than before. Not filled with tension or unsaid words.

"You hungry?" Mom asked.

She wrapped her arm around my shoulder; I thought that maybe this would be okay, and somehow, all this could end in a good way. "Very," I said.

48.

Graham

CASSIE. CASSIE. CASSIE.

Sitting in my apartment reminded me of her and last night. I lay awake all night thinking about her. I usually did, but it was more intense. Where I was usually awake, angry or confused, last night I was awake with thoughts of her touching me. Her pressed against the wall. Her hands on my chest. Her lips on mine, her hands roaming, my body's response, the look on her face before she left. Every thought of her made my heart race faster.

My phone rang, and I thought it was Cassie, but it was Molly. "I'm downstairs," she said.

"Come up," I said.

"You come down."

I opened the door and I started to talk, but she turned away and lowered herself on the single step outside my front door. I gulped down my nerves.

"I have a question," she said before I could speak. I sat next to her, but as soon as I did she stood and blocked the afternoon sun from my face. "Just one question."

I nodded.

"Have you been in love with her since the beginning of our relationship, or was it just because she came back?"

"What?"

Molly's hands moved around in the air while she spoke, and her words were fast. Almost running into each other. "Because I've been thinking about it. I was either a way for you to try to move on from her, or I was more than that and when you saw her it all came rushing back. Which one?"

I rolled my neck. "Both? I didn't know I still loved her until she came back. And now—"

"Now you want her."

I nodded slowly. Was that what I wanted? Yes. I think it was. "I'm sorry. I swear I—"

"Didn't mean it, I know. I should've run as soon as you told me about her, or when I learned you saved her mom, but I liked you," she said. "You were cute and funny and you made me feel..." She paused. "I never should've stayed."

"Molly."

She shook her head. "I've been there for you since the very beginning. I was patient. I listened, but I'm never going to be the girl next door. I'm Molly, not Cassie, and I can't be with you when you're in love with her. I won't. I'm not second best, and I refuse to settle for that with my man. I sacrifice enough for other people."

"You deserve so much more than I can give you. You should have that guy who feels so crazy in love with you that he can't breathe."

Molly nodded slowly. "The way you feel about her?"

I didn't respond, but I didn't need to. We both

knew the answer already. There were no other words between us, and she turned away and walked down the path back to her car. The last I saw of her was the sun bouncing off her blonde hair.

49.

Cassie

FOUR DAYS AGO I kissed Graham. I hadn't seen
him since. Not in passing or a text. I'd been thinking
a lot since that night. Maybe he was right about all of
it. I was selfish, and we were wrong, and there was no
future for us. Even if I thought I wanted it.

Dr. Lambert had been helpful. She told me to find
the thing that gives me passion. I wasn't sure where
to start, but I kept listening to June's music. Buying
things on iTunes and ordering new vinyls. There was
some good music out there. I was writing more lyrics
than I knew had existed inside of me. Somewhere
in all the thinking, in the debating about Graham, in
watching Rohan's song hit number one on the charts,
and in listening to my heart, I found my path. It only
took four days, give or take a few years.

I clicked send on my seventh application to a label
internship. This one was for producing. I wasn't really
sure where in music my heart lied, but I knew it was,
and had always been, for me. I'd had a lot of free time
to research while I waited for Graham.

My phone rang, and it was June. "I knew you'd be awake."

"I am. You made it?"

"Yesterday. Then I slept for fourteen hours. What are you doing? Miss me yet?"

I clicked a new tab on my computer. "Applying to internships."

June gasped. "Internships? Little Cassie found a path? What is it?"

I paused. "Music."

"I bet you feel like an idiot now."

I laughed. I guessed I did; I thought it would ruin me, like it did my parents, but it really saved Mom. At least for a while. "It's the only thing that has ever made me happy."

"And Graham."

I sighed. I still didn't know if there was a place for our feelings or my happiness. "He hasn't even talked to me since."

"He will. You have to make him want to be," she said. "I forgot how fucking sunny it is in LA."

"I have no remorse for you," I said with a smile.

"So, if you get one of these internships, what happens?"

"I don't know if I can even leave Mom again. What if something happens? She needs me. I probably won't get picked anyway. We'll see." I'd take it one thing at a time. I couldn't abandon her this time, and I couldn't lose myself either.

"I don't think your mom would want you to stay," June said.

"We'll see," I said, but I didn't feel hopeful. "Go enjoy your sunshine."

"Yes. Gotta track down some hot celebs or something! Bye, Harlen."

50.

Graham

I **PUSHED SEND** on the last of my forms for Rice. I had a schedule, loans to pay until I die, and a roommate. This was happening. Two months until I started my own life. I closed the computer and saw a light across the yard from Cassie's room. I was being an ass, I knew that, but I didn't know what to say to her. I didn't have anything to offer her; I was moving. She wasn't going to stay here, and neither was I. We couldn't be anything.

Someone pounded on my door, and I knew, pretty much immediately, that it was Cassie. No one else would be here at two in the morning.

I bolted down the stairs and sure enough, she was in front of me. Her hair sticking up all over the place, and getting longer like the Cassie I used to know.

"I'm sorry," she said. "I'm really, really sorry."

With the words, her voice cracked a little. Cass didn't cry.

"Come inside," I said, opening the door for her. She shook her head.

"I was wrong. When I left you. You haven't asked me about it since I've been home, but I want you to know. I need you to know, Graham, that I loved you. That I still love you."

I stared at her for a moment. We were really doing this at 2 a.m. "Let's at least sit."

I closed the door and we sat on the wicker couch on my parents' back porch. She hesitated for a moment before moving past me. My mind was racing with questions, and my heart was a jackhammer out of control. I really wanted to touch her, but I also knew I should keep my hands to myself. This was confusing enough, and she came here for a purpose. One I wanted to know, too. I was barely seated when she turned back to face me.

"I know I was wrong."

I swallowed. Did I really want to hear this?

"This doesn't make it right, but I was scared."

"Of me? Of us? What?" My voice was low because I couldn't decide what I felt. Angry or disappointed or sad. All of the above.

Cassie shook her head. "Not you—never you. Not even us, because I needed us. You were all I knew that was real, and I would never have survived without us. Without you." She paused and stood, moving around again. She couldn't sit still. Was she really that nervous? "I was scared of myself."

I didn't know what to say. This whole thing was a lot to process. The last week had been a crazy whirlwind. Ever since she'd come back, really. I didn't know up from down.

Cass bit the side of her cheek, and looked off into space. As she spoke, her hands twisted around her shirt. "I had all these acceptance letters to schools all over the country. I knew you'd go wherever I wanted, but I didn't get to tell you. Then, you asked me to marry you and I told myself that we could have it all. I could go to school, you could go to school, and we could be married. I wanted it, I really did."

She sat again on the edge of the wicker couch, so close I could've shifted a little right and our knees would've touched. I told myself to breathe, because this was the part I'd been wondering for a year. The part that I didn't have the courage to ask about.

"We'd been gone all that weekend, and I picked up some of Mom's favorite éclairs to bring with me."

I'd kept her busy those few days. I still remembered them like they were yesterday. We were together, completely happy and alone in those three days in a cabin in the mountains. Happy and alone and engaged.

"I was going to tell her about the engagement, like I said I would, but when I got home she was in a manic state." Cassie pushed a piece of hair behind her ear. It was just long enough now to stay there. "Mom talked to me like I was someone else. Not Cassie; Cassie was a baby. A friend. She kept saying she wanted my dad back. She wanted him back. I said he was dead, and she said he wasn't, that he left because he couldn't handle being with her and her mood swings. She said she ruined his life."

Her dad. All this happened because of her dad? *Shit.* "Cassie—"

"It was all I could think about for days, Graham," she said. Her hands wandered along her legs, and I couldn't look away from her face. Her voice cracked and I had to fight the urge to touch her, to comfort her. "I had your ring on my finger, and you were promising me yourself forever. I wanted that—you have to know I wanted that—but what if I got sick? We were young; we are young. There were no clues about what could

225

happen, but I felt like, for months, like I was losing it."

Around us, everything was quiet. Even the cicadas were listening to this moment. She thought I would leave her, so she left me. That logic made no sense.

"I would never leave you," I whispered after a pause.

"I know," she said. She smiled lightly, but I wasn't smiling. I was confused. If she knew then why leave? "That was the thing: you would stay. You would take care of me the same way I had to take care of my mom. That sucked for me, and I hated her for it, and I didn't want to ruin your life that way, Graham."

Even as she said it, a tear fell down her face. She didn't get it. I closed that little space so our knees bumped. I couldn't believe that was why she left.

"I couldn't live with myself if I did that. So I left you. I thought I was saving you. I did it for you," Cassie said.

"A life without you? That's harder. I woke up and you were gone. Gone. No note, no phone calls, nothing. Do you know what that was like for me?" My voice sounded a little bitter, angrier, than I wanted it to. But she left. All of this separation was because of something that could've been cleared up with a conversation. If she would've trusted me enough to tell me this before, then we'd be together right now. Right now we'd have a life together, somewhere else, instead of being here like this.

God, if I would've said something sooner. She'd stood there the day I went after her and admitted she loved me, but she kept saying she wasn't good for me. She'd said she would hurt me. I should've known something was wrong. I should've seen it when she looked at me. It was our language, the words beyond words. I'd missed it.

"I'm sorry. I know that doesn't mean anything, but

I am. I never wanted to hurt you." Her voice was low, and she nestled her legs under her.

"What about when I came to school?" I asked.

Seeing her there that day felt like waking up without her all over again. My heart didn't know what to do. I'd felt it all at once. The love for her, the anger, the disappointment, the doubt. I'd half expected her to run into my arms like in those movies, but she hadn't. She'd lingered a few feet away from me, and we'd stared at each other. All the words I'd planned to say drifted away, and that's when I saw the look was in her eyes, the one that I'd known so well. The one that I'd hated, filled with uncertainty and fear. I should've known. I did know, but I didn't want to see it. I'd been stubborn. I didn't want to let her go, to admit that she was lost, and that I was lost.

I'd still loved her when she gave me back that ring, just like I still loved her now. I wish I didn't anymore, that I could let go. She'd left me. That should've been enough. But ten years of being Graham and Cassie wasn't easy to give up on. She'd taught me how to be that stubborn, and until I'd left that school with nothing but a ring and a broken heart, I didn't know how much I'd needed that lesson.

Cassie stared at the ground like it was the most interesting thing in the whole fucking messed up world. Everything was quiet, too quiet. "That killed me. I never expected you to come. I didn't leave my room for a week after you left," she said.

That didn't make up for what happened. I'd been there. I'd laid my heart out for her, and she turned me away. She told me to leave, to move on. She said we wouldn't work—and all that time, she'd loved me. We'd wasted all of it.

"Why not tell me? I knew there was something else

going on, but you wouldn't tell me."

Cassie stood up again, her arm brushing against mine as she did. "Would it have mattered? If I had told you I was scared, you would've stayed anyway. I thought through every scenario and the one constant in all of them was you."

I didn't want to hear that shit. Not after all we'd been through. She could've told me something real, instead of that "she wasn't good for me" shit. That was the worst about all of it. That hurt the most because since when had I not been enough for her?

"You trying to save me—you should've talked to me, Cassie." But how many times had I done the same thing? Tried to protect her without her knowing. And how many problems had it caused?

"I know." Cassie picked at her fingernails, barely looking at me.

"Did you even think about what it was doing to me? To think that you didn't want me after all that we'd been through?" I wanted to stop talking because I could tell it was hurting her, but all the words kept rushing out. All the things I hadn't said, and had wanted to say. Once I admitted one of them to myself, they were all too big to ignore. "I felt like shit. Like less than shit. I wanted to hate you. I really did, but I couldn't. I loved you. I loved you and I knew there was something else. I knew it."

I never should have let her go. I should've fought harder, and then maybe...

Cassie froze in front of me. "I thought you would be happier without having to worry about me. To wait for me. To follow me. I thought you could find your own life, one without me. I thought you would be better off."

Tears streamed from her eyes, and she was close

enough that I could pull her near. This girl who I knew I still loved despite all this stuff she was telling me. I'd only seen Cassie cry once in all our years together. She was always so strong, so together. She didn't like to show weakness, and here she was baring her soul to me. I reached out and took her hand. She looked at me again, and I saw her. Really saw her. She was still scared, but underneath all that, there was something she didn't have before. Maybe in all the years I'd known her, there was hope.

She left her hand in mine, and I stroked the top of it with my finger. "I didn't tell you all this to convince you to love me again. I know you've started over; I know I hurt you. I just wanted you to know—you deserved to know. It was never you. It was easier to run away from the things I was afraid of, instead of facing them. I'm not brave like you."

I shifted in the seat so I was facing her. "What? That's crazy." I wasn't brave. I had done things, kept things from her, from myself. I led Molly on because I didn't want to face my feelings. That wasn't something someone brave did.

She laced her fingers with mine, and my whole body exhaled at the movement. "I know you saved my mom from the fire."

I opened my mouth and closed it again. How did she know that?

A small smile was on the corner of Cassie's mouth. "Molly told me. Mom verified. Why did you tell me it was Mrs. Pearson?"

I stretched my arm across my knee, careful not to disrupt our hands. I didn't want to let go now that she was linked to me again. "I thought if you didn't know it was me, you'd come back. I didn't want you to stay away because of me, or to come back because of me. I wanted you to come back for her. For yourself."

"Part of me did come back for you. You're always part of everything I do, Graham."

I didn't expect her to say that, and it lifted something inside me. Who was this girl? If she could be honest, I had to be honest. "That phone call was difficult. I didn't want to face you. I'm not as brave as you think I am."

She shook her head. "That's not true."

We stared at each other for what felt like hours, but it was only seconds. Only a few beats of my heart. I felt my body leaning in toward her, feeding off the bond between us. I looked at her lips, and wanted to taste them again. I leaned in toward her, and she started to do the same. I wanted all this stuff between us to be in the past, and I wanted her.

But Cassie pulled her hand from mine, and kissed my cheek quickly. "Thank you for saving my mom."

51.

Cassie

I WOKE UP the next afternoon and my head felt like a weight. Crying did that. I'd played last night in my head a million times, but it never ended that way. With me walking away. In my scenarios, it was Graham kissing me. It was never just over. I guess I'd gotten my wish for Graham to be free of me. That was for the best, anyway. We weren't the same people we used to be. There was no sense in telling myself we could rebuild that and go back.

There was no going back in life. Only forward.

I was ready for that.

I curled up on the porch with some coffee and my notebook. Even though an internship felt like an impossibility since someone had to help my mom, I still had music in some way. There were a lot of songs in my head, and I started writing them down. Lyric after lyric. Maybe this could be my future.

It's your life // it's your call // you can't be afraid/ of the fall // If you want to fly // you've gotta try // close your eyes // let it go // Hold on tight

Or the start of one.

⌀⌀⌀

I WENT DOWNSTAIRS for lunch, and the kitchen table was covered in papers. I called out for Mom, but there was no reply. I picked one of the pages and there was a picture of a woman with a smile.

Qualifications: Graduated 1978 from Duke. Twenty years of Nursing Experience in general medicine. Ten years in North Carolina State Psychiatric Medicine. Daughter with Down syndrome.

Looking for: Low-key patients who need daily assistance at their homes. Will live in.

"Cassie! You're up! Coffee?" Mom said, bouncing into the room.

"What's this?" I asked, waving the sheet in the air.

She took a sip from her mug. "A resume."

I knew that. "For what?"

She went into the kitchen and poured me a cup of coffee. "I'm hiring a nurse."

"A nurse?"

"A companion, maybe. I like that term better. Someone who can be here to make sure I'm making good choices and to be part of things." Mom handed me the mug, a smile on her face.

"You don't need a nurse. I'm here."

Mom reached her hand out and rubbed it on my back. "You have things to do, Cassie. You can't stay here."

"What? Don't be silly." I was here. I was staying. It was already done. Mom needed me, and I'd already decided to give her that.

She lowered herself into a chair, turning through

a few of the resumes. "I heard you on the phone with June." She smiled when she glanced up at me. "I want you to go and do whatever you want to do."

"Mom," I started.

Mom shook her head. "Music is exciting! I knew that was where you'd end up. You have such an ear for it—have since you were a baby. We used to sing to you and you'd dance along in our laps. You loved when Richard would play Bruce Springsteen."

I took a seat next to her. "I'm here, Mom. I don't want to go back to Butler."

"Then don't. Go wherever you want!" She took my hand. "The point is that we both know you don't need to be here. Follow your dreams, Cassie. I've already had mine, and I can take care of myself. I know you think I can't, which is why I'll have someone else move in. Maybe not forever, but for as long as I feel like I need it."

She was serious. My mom was going to have a stranger come live in her house so I didn't have to. I never expected that. I was so resigned to stay here after the other day. "I don't know what to say."

"My life doesn't have to be yours, and I don't want it to be," she said. "Having someone here will be nice. This house is too lonely anyway."

I hugged her. She rubbed my back and held me close. It was hard to believe this was my mom. She was so grown up. "Can I help?" I asked.

"Only for an hour. Then you have to apply to more internships or schools or whatever you want."

"Deal." My mom had her moments of being the best. This was definitely one of them. I reached for a stack of resumes. "So the most important question—favorite Stevie Nicks song?"

"Of course," Mom laughed.

TWO HOURS LATER, we'd narrowed it down to four nurses for an interview next week and I'd applied to a couple more internships. It felt good, for the first time, like it could actually happen.

Like somehow I could really find something to make me happy.

50.

Graham

"WHAT ARE YOU doing, son?" Dad asked me. He'd been away on business for seven weeks, flying back and forth between home and New York and Hong Kong. I didn't realize he was back. He was still dressed in his suit, rolling his suitcase right behind him.

"You home for good?"

Dad smiled, but he looked tired. "I had to spend some time with my boy before he went to school."

"James helped me load up my truck with this. I have something to fix," I said, answering his other question.

Dad eyed the wood on the back of the truck. "Looks familiar." He paused, but I didn't answer. I didn't have to. He knew this project. "Where you taking it?"

"Garage."

"Let me help you," Dad said. He threw his jacket on the ground next to his suitcase and climbed up into the bed of the truck. "Glad it's going to be fixed."

Dad took one end of the wooden beams, and I took the other. I was glad, too. Cassie wasn't the only one who'd made mistakes. I couldn't let her think she was.

$$\mathcal{co}\,\mathcal{O}\,\mathcal{o}$$

MY ALARM WENT off at 1 a.m. I grabbed a bottle of water, put on my shoes, and started unloading my tools. Each trip back and forth, I glanced up at Cassie's room. The light was off. *It will work out.* But I wasn't fully convinced. This could be the dumbest plan in history. I didn't have a Plan B yet.

I took a long swig of my water, and started moving the pieces of wood I'd cut earlier in the day. I had to do the short ones first. I moved toward the broken fence, and measured a foot on my tape measure. When I found the right place, I put a marker in the ground. I went all the way around and marked until I ran out of room. I hoped this was the right decision, but there was no turning back now.

An hour later, I was ready.

I dug at that marker with my shovel, digging up bits of the ground, and when it was big enough, I shoved the first wooden beam into the ground, hammered until it was solid, and then re-positioned the dirt. After the second beam, I started on the first long side of the fence.

Cassie hated surprises, but I was thinking of this more as a grand gesture.

I got one side done before Cassie's light came on and I smiled.

51.

Cassie

I FOLLOWED THE pounding outside. Immediately, I noticed that every light in Graham's apartment was on, and he was in the space between our yards, re-building the fence.

"What are you doing?" I asked, moving closer toward him.

He pushed his foot down on the shovel, and glanced up at me. He was quiet for a moment, staring at me, and then he said, "Fixing what I broke."

"The fence?"

He shrugged. "To start."

My nerves tingled. There was a hidden meaning in his words. I started to say something but Graham went back to work, and I debated what to do. I couldn't sleep now, not when I knew he was out here working. So, I went toward the old part, a few feet off where he was, and sat on the top. I tightened my robe around myself, and tried to cover up my thighs.

Graham raised an eyebrow at me. "You're staying?"

"Do you mind me staying?"

"No," he said with a smile.

I sat, and watched him work. Sat and debated what was supposed to happen next. I'd cleared the air, and moving forward was next, but what were we moving toward?

"There wasn't a storm," Graham said as he moved some logs around. "Well, maybe Hurricane Tucker."

I smiled. "I figured."

His lip twitched and he turned back to work before I could see his face, but I knew he was smiling. I twisted the tie on my robe around my wrist. "Why are you doing this in the middle of the night?"

"I haven't slept well lately," he said.

"It's been hard for me since I got back, too."

"It's been hard for me since you left," Graham said. His eyes locked on mine.

Way to say stupid things, Cassie. "Sorry." I should've stopped bringing it up if I ever wanted to move on.

"You can stop apologizing," he said.

"I can?"

Graham nodded. "We all do stupid shit that we think is right, Cassie."

"Is that forgiveness?" I fought back the smile I felt forming. This was what I wanted, his forgiveness.

"I think it is," he said. He doesn't look back at me, but I don't need him to. I believe him.

A weight lifted off me in that moment, and even though it was good and wonderful, I wondered if I deserved it. At the end of the day, I'd still made my decisions. If he could forgive me, really forgive me, then I could let him go. It wasn't what I wanted, but it was right and the most fair to him.

"Graham," I said. Even just saying his name made my heart hurt. Fairness sucked.

"Cass?"

I took a breath. "I'm happy for you. Really, I am."

"Happy about what?" he asked, unloading a little dirt to the side. He looked at me again.

It was harder to say with him staring at me.

"You were the only good thing about this place for me, and I'm glad you're getting out. You have a good girlfriend and a future at the school of your dreams. I'm happy that you have what you want." After I said it, I realized how much I really meant it. All I wanted was him happy.

He froze for a moment, and I was nervous. Then, Graham threw the shovel and he lowered a beam into the hole he'd dug. "We broke up."

"What?"

"Molly and I—we broke up." His eyes were intense on me.

"Oh..." I started. "I'd apologize, but you told me to stop."

I swear he smiled.

"It's okay. It was a good thing," he said.

Such a little phrase, but for some reason, it took my breath away.

52.

Graham

SHE WAS RIGHT next to me, but she was so quiet. It was almost like she was afraid to breathe. I could feel the tension around her, and I wondered if she could hear my heart pounding in the silence. I did all this to get her out here—and now here she was.

"You're wrong about one thing," I said, pounding the next post into the ground.

"What's that?"

"I'm not happy." I hit the beam again. "And I don't have everything that I want." One more swing and then my eyes were on her. "I don't have you."

I threw the hammer to the ground, and it was an instant. She leapt from the fence into my arms, and wrapped her legs around my waist. I couldn't think about anything else except how much I wanted to taste every inch of her.

I lowered Cass to her feet, and she broke our kiss, inhaling a half-laugh, half-breath. I smiled. This was our moment. Everything was out there and now we could be whatever we wanted. I kissed her again, and her body pressed against mine like it belonged there.

Cass guided me toward the door of my apartment, and opened it. Then, I remembered the one thing. I pulled her to a stop. "Wait—I need to tell you something."

She shook her head and kissed me. I leaned into it and welcomed her tongue into my mouth. This girl couldn't get close enough. She caught my lip with her teeth playfully. "No more talking."

Okay.

53.

Cassie

BY THE TIME we were up the stairs, my lips were already in that swollen, numb, but this-was-so-good-don't-stop phase. Graham closed the door behind us, and for a moment, it was hard to believe this was happening. Everything wasn't totally lost. He turned back to me and my heart was pounding as he slipped the robe off my shoulders, and placed a kiss under my ear, on my neck, on my collarbone. He feathered kisses down my jaw to my ripe lips, and opened them with his tongue. I practically purred as our mouths clung in a heated kiss.

My hands slid up his shirt, pulling it over his head, not wanting to separate. I ran my hands down his chest and his abs, and his lips moved to my neck. His hand slid under my shirt and over my skin, leaving chills. He eased my shirt over my head and his fingers trailed over my breasts. His hands were like ice as he touched me and made every nerve inside me shiver. I never wanted that to stop.

His lips and tongue flitted over my nipples; I braced

my arms around him so I didn't fall over. I moaned as he moved his lips up my breasts, back to my waiting mouth. His tongue explored, and his hands continued to caress my breasts. My body was feeling everything, everywhere, a thousand pins and needles. I let him lead me, let his tongue and his hands and his breath take me away.

My fingers fumbled to unbutton his pants without stopping the kissing, and his pants fell to the floor. My hand went downward into his boxers, and as I took the full length of him in my hand he parted from my mouth with a gasp. I smiled at the reaction. Graham kissed me again quickly before flashing a devilish smile. He pulled off my shorts, kissing my thighs as he lowered the fabric. He did the same with my underwear and his fingers slid inside me. My breath hitched at the sudden entry, and got more ragged as he moved inside me. I whispered his name and gripped his shoulders. I was going to come undone. I moaned as his fingers found my clit and pressed myself against him. He kissed me as he moved deeper and harder inside me while I groaned into his mouth.

I couldn't think anymore. My legs felt weak as I leaned my whole body against him. He ran his tongue along my neck, and I moaned his name, pressing my mouth into his shoulder as my fingers dug in for something to steady me. He was the only thing keeping me standing.

"Come for me," he said breathlessly in my ear. I whispered his name while my body uncoiled around him, and then, he kissed me again and lowered me to the floor.

He was on top of me, the pressure of his erection pressing into my hip, while my hands explored him and our mouths breathed in each other. I was safe under him, like nothing could ever harm me. I was always that way when I was with him. There was nothing and no one who would ever be able to complete me like he could.

Graham looked down at me. "You're the most beautiful woman I've ever known." He pressed a kiss to my collarbone. "I will never stop wanting you."

"I need you," I said, wrapping my arms around his neck and pulling him in for another kiss. "Now."

I felt him enter me slowly, and I bit his bottom lip. He was the same as I remembered, filling me perfectly, impossibly full, but my body felt different around him. As if I had a few million extra nerve endings and he knew how to trigger each one of them. Maybe I was new or different, or maybe it was him. Maybe it was us. Whatever it was, the feeling of him inside me was almost too much.

He moved inside me and my fingers ran down his back. I felt myself already building and we'd barely gotten started. My body craved him too much. "God, Graham."

He moved harder. I lifted my hips into his movements, and we both moaned together. The sounds grew louder between us, and I focused on him moving inside me. It was all I'd wanted for months, and I'd never thought I could actually have it again. I moaned loudly in tune with him as coherent thought deserted me and I floated on pure sensation. For a brief moment, time stopped, and we were caught in the middle, frozen together as one.

Graham

I KISSED DOWN Cass's throat to the full rise of her breasts, as she snuggled up beside me and intertwined her legs with mine. My whole body was exhausted, and alive, and hungry for her, and my hands couldn't leave her alone. I kissed every inch of her that I could find and enjoyed the sounds she made under me. The sounds I'd missed and couldn't get enough of. I didn't want her to ever stop making them.

Then she laughed. I really loved her laugh.

"You shouldn't laugh after sex, Cass. You'll give a guy a complex."

That only made her laugh more. I gave her my best stern face, but I couldn't be mad at her. Not after that. After this.

"We didn't even make it to the bed," she said with a smile. "I can literally touch it."

She reached out her hand over her head, and sure enough, it was right there.

"And that's funny?"

"I didn't really imagine this on the floor. Like we're animals."

"I imagined it everywhere," I said.

She smiled. "Everywhere?"

I nodded and kissed her neck. "The floor." Another kiss. "Your car." Another kiss. "The bed of my truck—"

"Why have we never done that?"

"The beach, the yard, against that stupid fence, a road somewhere." I kissed a new part of her body between each word, and then looked at her and couldn't stop smiling. "With you is all that matters to me."

"I don't deserve you," she said. I kissed her again, and she ran her hand down my face. "I really don't."

"No, you really don't," I said.

She hit me playfully on the arm. "I love you, Graham Tucker."

"I love you, too. Always."

I kissed her again, and her body burnt this path against mine. My body groaned in response to her hand, which was suspiciously drifting downward. "You want to be an animal again?" I whispered in her ear.

"You could convince me," she said. I gasped as her hand moved against me, and her eyes widened with laughter. I was so hard under her touch, even after what we'd just done. I couldn't get enough of her. I inhaled some air, exhaled her name, as Cass took control of my body.

54.

Graham

SHE SEEMED SO happy next to me in the morning sunlight—I hadn't seen her that way in a very long time. I folded my hands behind my head and looked at her. I wanted to capture that moment and keep it forever. To imprint it on my memory as a reminder that these rare times of pure bliss—those were the moments, the days, we existed for. Those were the ones that kept us moving forward, kept us fighting and forgiving, and loving. Every mistake, every stupid decision, every lie found hope in this. We'd found our way back to each other, and I never wanted to forget.

"Why are you staring at me?"

"Because you're beautiful."

Her face lit up, and I loved that I could still make her blush. She was the same Cass, the same and new and completely different at once. I patted the bed, and she lay back down next to me, resting her head in that spot on my chest. It was made for her.

"I keep thinking about this thing," Cassie said slowly.

"You can think of something besides a whole year

of make-up sex?"

I couldn't see her face, but I knew she was blushing again. "What thing?" I kissed her head.

"You remember that thing you always say to me? *You can't live your life in fear or you'll never live.* This reminds me of that."

I took a deep breath. That thing.

"How so?" I asked.

"I don't know. I guess it just makes sense now. I was so afraid, and I wasted all this time."

"You don't have to waste any more of it," I said.

She *hmmed*, and I knew that sound. It urged something up in the pit of my stomach. Cassie knew something, or she thought she did, and she may have been evolving, but she was still her. Any ideas she had would spiral. She would over-analyze them and they would make her doubt. I didn't want to be the thing she doubted. Not ever.

"I should tell you something about that."

"About what?" she asked.

"That saying. I almost told you before, but then..." *You pulled me upstairs.* I sat up, and she faced me. I smiled at her one more time because I loved to see that glow on her face when I did. "This is a new start for us, so I don't want to have any secrets."

I locked eyes with her. This was harder than I thought it would be. "I heard that from your father."

She frowned. "You didn't know my father. I don't even know my father."

I shook my head, and took a breath. "I met him once."

"Met who?"

"Your father," I said.

Cassie blinked, confused, and then shook her head. "That's not funny."

I gulped. This was it. My secret. The thing I tried to protect her from knowing, and it's the cause of so many problems. "I'm not kidding. I met him. Richard Harlen. He had your eyes," I said. She bunched the sheet over her chest. Her hair fell around her face when she moved, and a lump formed in my throat. I rose next to her. "He showed up at the hospital after you found your mom in the bathtub. We'd been there all night and they finally let you in to see her."

That was hard for her, for us both. We hadn't known what was happening or why. They wouldn't really tell Cassie much. I'd waited outside the door, sitting in one of those hard, plastic chairs that existed only in emergency rooms—even though that's where they should've been the most comfortable since people at hospitals had to almost live in them.

"I heard someone talking at the nurse's station, a man with a low voice, and he was standing fifty feet away. I'd only seen him in pictures, but I knew it was him."

Cassie stared at me in disbelief while I talked. I wanted to know what she was thinking. This was going to kill her. I didn't want to lose her, but not telling her the whole truth again was going to make that happen anyway.

"I didn't know what to do. I only thought of you, Cass. I didn't know how you'd handle him being there on top of everything. I didn't even think, really."

"What'd you say to him?" she asked, her voice low.

Richard Harlen looked me up and down when I'd introduced myself. "Well, I said, 'With all due respect, sir, why are you here?'"

"You what?" Cassie shook her head.

"He said they'd called him because he was the emergency contact."

Cassie wasn't looking at me, but I knew I had to tell her. I was wrong to have never told her anyway.

"I told him I was with you," I said. To his benefit, the man had looked a little taken aback by her name. He'd at least paused, and I had no clue what I was doing, but I knew she wouldn't be able to see him. I couldn't protect her from the stuff with her mom, but that, her father, I could. So I had. "I told him he had to leave."

"What do—"

"I told him it wasn't fair to you for him to be there." Cassie shook her head at me. "I said he would make it all harder on you, and you didn't deserve that. I said he couldn't help, not now, and that you didn't even know he was alive."

Her father hadn't seemed surprised by the confession. He'd been silent, processing. I knew he'd bail. I knew it. I could sense it.

"Then what?" Cassie asked, after a few minutes of silence.

I nodded. "I asked why he was there. Why hadn't he come on your birthday or one of the Christmases where you asked about him, or any of the times Mrs. H was sick. I asked him how he could leave you. He said I didn't know what he'd been through with Mrs. H, or how hard it was to leave." Cassie started to speak, but I didn't let her. "I told him he was right, but I knew how easy it was to stay." She looked at me, her eyes wide and sparkling with tears. "I said he could come back the next day, but that right then it was too much. I told him I was trying to protect you, and that you were dealing with enough."

"You love her?" he'd asked me.

"Yes, sir."

"Is she happy?" he'd asked.

"With Cassie, you never really know," I'd said.

He'd smiled, like it was a joke that I missed out on. "I reckon you're right. It's a lot to throw at a girl. Maybe tomorrow, you say?"

I'd nodded. "Maybe tomorrow." He didn't come back the next day. I'd known he wouldn't. He'd already proven he wasn't the type to stay.

I looked at Cassie. "He said he'd come back later, and he asked me to do him a favor." Cassie didn't speak, but she waited, her eyes wide. "'Tell her not to live her life in fear or she'll never really live.' I told him that he could tell you that when he came back. But he didn't come back."

The room was silent. Cassie wasn't facing me anymore, and I reached out to touch her but she flinched away.

"Say something, Cass."

"Four years you've known?" Her voice was strangely calm. She was trying, but I knew she was upset.

"Yes," I said.

She spun around to face me. "Why wouldn't you tell me that?" She shook her head, like she couldn't believe I'd done it. She'd done the same thing, but in another way. We were more alike than we probably even knew. "He came for us, Graham."

I took her hand, even though she didn't want me to. She had to see me, to hear me. "He left again, Cassie. He would've always left. He wouldn't have been able to be what you needed."

"But maybe I would've!" she yelled, pushing away from me again and moving off the bed.

She was crying and it threw me off. "If I hadn't learned about my dad the way I did, maybe I would never have freaked out! Maybe I would've stayed and all of this last year wouldn't have happened."

"You don't know any of that is true, Cass," I said, moving with her. I grabbed her waist and pulled her, but she didn't budge. "What else would it have done to your life? You don't know; I don't know. Maybe you didn't leave; maybe you did. It doesn't matter now. We can't change it."

I'd tried to look him up for her once before. I'd figured that the nurses got him so his number must be the same, but it was disconnected. It was like the man re-disappeared. She didn't need to know all that, though. Not right now.

"It does matter, Graham. It will always matter. You met him and I haven't."

I knew then that it wasn't my secret that hurt, it was his. It was that he was alive and stayed away. It was him not wanting to see his own daughter. I could see the pain on her face, the rejection. I could see it because I'd known it.

Cassie moved around the living room in my small studio. She threw on her robe.

"What are you doing?" I asked.

"I need some air," she said.

No, no, no. This wasn't happening. I bolted from the bed and grabbed her arm. "Don't walk away right now. Let's talk about this."

Her eyes were full of tears. She couldn't leave again. She couldn't walk out on us. "Cass," I said. I pressed my forehead against hers. She stayed there for a second next to me as tears fell from her eyes.

"I need some air," she said. "Just for a minute."

"Okay," I said.

And then she went toward the door. I let her go this time, because maybe that was the problem before. I'd held on too tight. I'd proposed too early. I was too scared to let her have space and find herself because

252

if she did that then maybe she'd find herself away from me. I didn't know who I was without Cassie, so I thought giving her that ring would mean she'd always stay, when really, it made her run.

55.

Cassie

I DIDN'T MAKE it any farther than the steps of his apartment before I couldn't stop crying. I wasn't mad at Graham—I was mad at myself. I'd tried so hard not to be like my mom, not to let her illness or her way of living be my own, that I turned myself into my father. Into someone who couldn't handle the bipolar, someone too afraid to live, someone who left. Mom was more consistent than him. Even when she was in a manic state or depressed, she was there. She'd never left me.

Graham had always been my constant, too. He'd done the right thing with my dad that day. Even though it fucking sucked. He had a point that my dad couldn't wait a day, let alone stay through all the ones that followed. I was wrong before to think Graham couldn't handle me being sick. I was the one who couldn't handle it.

Being with him forever scared me. I'd said I'd marry him because I loved him, and I wanted to be that person he wanted me to be, but Cassie Before didn't know herself at all. I was only just meeting myself.

How could I have been what he wanted me to be when I didn't know what I wanted?

I wiped my eyes because that Cassie was gone.

This Cassie was on her way to knowing what she wanted.

After a few more minutes, I went back upstairs. Graham was sitting on his couch, staring at the door. When I came in, he crossed the small space in a couple steps.

"I'm sorry," we both said at the same time.

"I want us to stop apologizing to each other. I don't blame you for my dad," I said. It wasn't everything I had to say, but right now I couldn't say it all to him. We could talk about it later. He reached out and wiped a tear off my cheek.

"I love you," he said. Then he kissed my cheek and closed the space between us. "I missed you."

My other cheek. "I want you."

My nose. "So much."

He pressed his lips against mine softly, and when he parted we were both smiling.

"You know what I want?" he whispered against my lips.

"What?"

"Food. I'm freaking starving."

"COME ON," GRAHAM said.

"I'm in my pajamas. Let me go home first," I said, but Graham led me toward his house anyway and into the kitchen. No one was there.

"I told you it would be fine," he said with a cocky

half-smile. He loved being right, and I rarely gave it to him. He could have this one.

"Look," he said, snatching a letter off the fridge. I moved toward him, and read it over.

Dear Son, Glad you are alive! You didn't come down for breakfast or lunch. Your father said he saw you last night for a few minutes; we went to dinner. Hopefully, we will see you in the morning? I whipped you up a little something and put it on the second shelf. See you later. Love, Mom and Dad.

P.S. Hi, Cassie.

"Oh my God, Graham!"

He laughed. "What's on the shelf I wonder?" He yanked the door open and started laughing some more. When he turned around, he held a huge stack of blackberry pancakes.

The same thing we ate the first time his parents found us together.

Mortifying.

"You're so cute when you blush," Graham said, kissing me again.

56.

Cassie

I STUMBLED HOME as the sun rose. The sky trailed with pinks and oranges, and it was the most beautiful morning. I stopped near the fence and took it in, and I could only smile. I was with Graham, and I was happy again. Whatever happened next with him going to school, I was happy. I walked toward my house and words played through my head.

The sky is falling but I don't care // Let it fall // I'm not scared at all // Nothing can hurt me when I'm with you // everything is brighter, life is renewed // you kiss me like there's no tomorrow // and if there's not then // I won't care // outside us it all falls apart // the world is lost, but you have my heart // the sky is falling and I'm not scared // I know how it feels // I'm falling too

Pieces of the world rain down // like snowflakes // like heartaches // it's the end of days // and I'm wrapped in you // where lights are brighter // seas are bluer // clouds will catch me // when they fall // your lips on mine // until the end of time // the sky is falling but I'm not scared // the sky is falling // let it fall // let it fall

I wrote it down as soon as I got into the house, and Mom greeted me, but I didn't want to forget any of it. When I was done, I looked up at her and noticed the smooth sound of Sinatra. Mom had a smile face that reminded me of June. "Another night at Graham's?"

I shrugged, closing the notebook. "Yeah."

"I bet you're tired."

"Mom!"

Mom laughed and held up her hands in defense. "June called ten minutes ago. Those were her words!"

June. I'd called her after the pancake incident two days ago, and before she'd even said "hello," her first words were, "You finally nailed that, didn't you?" The whole conversation was a downward slope of June-ness from there.

I joined Mom at the bar. "Did she say what she wanted? It's like 8 a.m. in LA. June isn't a morning person."

Mom shrugged. "She said she'd email you."

"Sorry, I haven't been here much."

Mom shook her head. "I was young and in love once," she said, moving through the house. I hadn't told her about Dad. I figured I'd ask Dr. Lambert first.

I poured myself some coffee and logged into my email. Three emails. One from June, one from the dean at Butler, and one from Yellow Stripe Records. Was this one of my internships? I hadn't applied to Yellow Stripe. I clicked on the email.

After reviewing your resume and receiving some highly recommended referrals per your application for a production internship with our label, we would love to schedule a phone interview.

I didn't apply here or send referrals. "Weird."

"What's wrong?" Mom asked.

I scanned the email again. This had to be a

mistake. "Yellow Stripe Records emailed me about an internship? I didn't send them any information."

"I know. I did."

I shot around in my chair to look at her. She did? "What?"

Mom lowered the page, and moved to stand next to me. "Well, June and I did. I spoke with her last week. That was fast! They must've liked you."

"Mom."

She reached over me and scrolled down on my laptop. "What?"

"What'd you do? Catch me up here."

Mom smiled. "I knew you wanted this, so I called June. We did the paperwork, and she and I found you some references, and she called her friend Rohan."

Rohan. He did that for me?

Mom continued, sitting next to me. "The current CEO is the daughter of an old client, so I made a call and mentioned that you applied. A bug in her ear, that's all music is anyway. A really great bug."

"You and June did this?"

"Catch up, Cassie. We did," Mom said. Her smile was bright and large. "So, now you have an interview. You're one step closer."

I didn't know what to say, so I did the only thing I could think of and hugged her.

A FEW DAYS later, I was in Dr. Lambert's office. I wasn't the same girl I had been a few days before. It was impossible to change overnight, yet parts of me had. The prospect of an internship, of a direction, was exciting, and Graham was the best of all.

"The interview went well?"

I nodded. "It did! They want me to come up in person in a couple weeks."

"You think this is something you'd enjoy?" she asked.

I smiled. Think wasn't the right word. "No, I know I'd love it."

"And what does Graham say?"

I shifted. "He's okay with it."

"Supportive?"

I didn't want to leave him, but we'd talked about this. A little, anyway. "It would be hard, but yes. He's very supportive."

"What aren't you telling me?"

How did she know that? It must've been some sort of superpower. I'd been thinking a lot about my father since Graham told me what happened.

"He met my father once," I started. Dr. Lambert leaned forward and I retold her the story Graham told me. She nodded, and stared at me intently.

"What's your response to that?"

"I was in shock, obviously."

"Were you angry?"

"A little, but I can't be mad at him for doing the exact same thing I did."

I could've sworn she smiled. "Which is?"

"I tried to protect him. He tried to protect me. We both ended up miserable because of it. I keep wondering what would have happened if he told me, you know? How things could have gone different ways."

"Does that make it easier?"

"No," I said. "More confusing."

"Do you want to know your father, Cassie?"

I paused. Yes. But he left. He left twice, and I didn't know if I could handle a third. We couldn't make people stay, no matter how much we wanted them to. This life wasn't for him, and I knew all about trying to fit a mold you couldn't fit into. "Part of me says yes; the other part thinks maybe it's better without him. What do you think?"

She lowered her hands into her lap. "I can't answer that for you. No one can except yourself."

"I figured."

There was nothing else to say about it right now.

Dr. Lambert took my silence and changed the subject. "How long until Graham has to leave for school?"

"Six weeks."

57.

Graham

I RAN MY FINGERS through Cass's hair. I slept better with her beside me. That fear of waking up alone, of losing something in my sleep that I couldn't hold on to that had plagued me every night, seemed to vanish now that she was back there beside me, and that she wanted to be there. I wanted her there forever. But right now, forever felt very close to ending.

It'd been three weeks since we made up, and in four weeks I was going to Texas. Neither of us had talked about school—or about the interview she flew to New York City for last week—but we both knew they were closing in on us.

Cassie stirred as I moved from the bed, but she didn't wake. I couldn't believe how quickly we fell back into a pattern of her and me, of us. It was like we were never apart. That was almost easy to believe, except we'd both grown. I felt it, and I saw it each time I looked at her. It was like she was rejuvenated, especially because she's had these interviews in the city. Purpose looked good on Cassie.

262

The morning sun poured through my window, and I glanced out at the half-fixed fence. I had spent more time with Cassie than I had on that fence. I had to finish it before I left. To leave something as a standing reminder of what we've been through to get wherever we ended up. I kissed Cassie's forehead and got the work boots out of my closet. I had a fence to finish.

∾၀ၒ

CASSIE NEVER LET me drive the convertible, so when she threw me the keys I knew our day out was more than a date at the beach. But I didn't question it, because Cassie did things in her own time. I knew that.

We found this little spot of empty sand where the shore and the grass started to come back together. We could see everything across the beach from there.

"It's a nice day," I said. "This was a good idea."

I kissed her neck twice before she turned into me and met my lips. For the moment, we took it slow, but then there was nothing slow about it. She was mine and I was hers, and there was no one else around to stop us or see us or separate us.

When we stopped for air, my whole body inhaled it. Soaked it up. Cass was a sponge and being with her seemed to steal parts of me. It was an intoxicating effect, one that had never gone away. Not since that first time I kissed her all those years ago at our fence.

"I got a call this morning," Cassie said.

I could feel this coming. This only meant one thing. "From the label?"

She smiled. "They want me."

"Shit, that's fantastic, Cass."

I meant it. I really wanted this for her. This was going to be good for her. She loved music. She'd always loved it—long before she loved me.

"I know. I'm excited."

She smiled, but I could tell she was sad. I could ignore that part for now. "What are the details?"

"They house me, pay me, and we take it six months at a time. Apparently, they loved me. They think I have the right spirit, whatever that means. Recommendations from Mom, one of my professors and Rohan didn't hurt."

I tensed a little at Rohan's name. In my head, there was never a Rohan. I didn't like thinking about Cass with another guy at all. Let alone a famous musician whose biggest hit was about her.

I kissed her quickly. She was going to be so good at this. I was trying to contain my excitement, but Cassie was made for music. "When do they want you?"

"Two weeks. I'll leave the day after you."

There it was. The real reason we were out here. We'd talked about this a lot. She wouldn't be happy if she followed me. I wouldn't have been happy if I tried to change my plans. We each had to find our own way.

"That's great, Cassie."

"Is it?" she asked, her big eyes staring up at me.

"Yes," I said.

"I don't want to leave you," she said. She looked down, biting the side of her cheek. This wasn't happening. She wasn't going to stand in her own way, not because of me.

I tilted her chin up to look at me. "You're going to New York. I'm going to Texas."

"We're going to be apart," she said.

"We knew it was coming."

"I just got you back, Graham."

I pushed down the sadness I felt. If she saw me upset, she'd be upset. She had to go. "We're not that far apart."

"Only New York and Texas."

"You always wanted an adventure. This is ours. Together."

She smiled and kissed me. I wanted to touch her as much as I could. When we parted, she rested her head on my shoulder. "What if you move there and meet a girl? What if you fall madly in love?"

"I am madly in love."

"With someone else."

She'd asked this question a few times already. I knew she loved me; she knew I loved her, but she had this fear of holding me back from something better. I didn't want anything better because it didn't exist.

"I won't," I said.

"You don't know that."

I chuckled. "What if you fall in love with some musician?"

She shoved me. "I'm serious. It could happen."

"I know."

And deep down, I did. Love was one thing, but life wasn't predictable. We couldn't map it out. I didn't want to think of ending up with anyone else.

"I don't want to be that couple that tried to make it work long distance and ended up hating each other," she said.

I sighed. "So what then?"

"I don't know."

"Me, either."

We were both quiet for a beat before I pulled her to her feet, and drug her into the ocean. I didn't have the answers either, but we had two weeks, and I was going to spend all of it with her.

58.

Cassie

I SHADED MY eyes from the setting sun and watched out the back door at Graham as he hammered another post into the ground. We were both leaving. Him in the morning; me tomorrow. It was a whole lot of uncertainty, and he was determined to finish that thing. Apparently, they were a lot harder to build than to destroy.

"That boy is working himself to death," Nora Jensen said, moving to stand next to me. "You should take him some water."

Nora was Mom's new roommate/nurse/ companion. She was a few years older than Mom, widowed with grown, married children in another state. She was bored, she'd said in her interview, and she wanted something exciting. When we asked her what her favorite Stevie Nicks song was, she didn't answer. Instead, she gave a full rundown about the differences in Stevie's solo work and in Fleetwood Mac and about the dynamics between Stevie, Christine McVie and Lindsay Buckingham. Well, she was pretty much a shoo-in.

I handed Graham a bottle of water, and he smiled at me, wiping some sweat from his brow.

"Almost done?"

He took a breath after gulping half the bottle. "Better—I'm finished."

"You did it."

The fence was nice. It was better than before. The back part was darkened from the original wood, and the new addition was brighter. It made me smile because he'd told me it was like us, and it sort of was. Old and New. Before and After.

"It took me too long. I kept getting distracted," he said, wrapping me in his sweaty arms. It was gross, but then he was kissing me and it didn't matter.

"This is new," I said, moving toward the swinging entrance.

"I thought this fence needed an adjustment. Now you can't threaten my life for crossing over since there's a door that swings both ways," he said.

"You're a genius," I said, kissing him again. I didn't want to stop doing that ever. "You should've thought of that years ago so it would've been easier to sneak into your house."

"That would've been brilliant," he said.

"Ten hours," I said.

"Then, let's not waste any more time," he said. He swooped me up in his arms, and carried me into his apartment. I knew Mom and Nora were probably watching, but I didn't even care.

I SAT ON the edge of Graham's bed and watched

him put the last of his things into a suitcase. This was it. This was the end. He was leaving. His whole apartment was empty and it was surreal. This was happening.

"Walk with me," he said, and I took his hand.

Outside, the sun had barely risen, but they were driving all the way to Texas. His parents were rushing around the kitchen, so Graham and I took a seat on the steps of his front porch. This was hard. Harder than leaving. Partial goodbyes.

"What are you thinking?" he asked me.

I ran my finger in circles over the back of his hand. "This is hard. I don't want to say goodbye."

"I don't either," he said, kissing the top of my head. "It's not goodbye, though. We'll talk tomorrow."

"And as much as we can, I know."

That was the decision we came to. Together. Graham and Cassie would be separate, free. He could do anything he wanted; I could do anything I wanted. We were going to be friends who were in love and separated. I wasn't his girlfriend, which he was against at first, but I was adamant. He'd never left; I had. I knew what it was like in a new place. We would Skype or talk on the phone and email, and we would see what happened. No expectations, no guilt.

"Have you changed your mind?" he asked.

I knew he meant the arrangement. "No. You?"

59.

Graham

THERE WERE A few days where Cassie thought she would come with me. And that thought was really appealing. Coming home to her every single day. But I wanted her to be happy, and music made her happy. Architecture made me happy. We had separate paths, and that was the thing I'd overlooked all along. I was so worried about keeping her close, about protecting her, that we pushed each other away. I wouldn't let that happen again.

"It's not what I want, but you're right," I said. I didn't really think she was and I really didn't want to be only her friend. We'd tried that and it didn't look good on us. I would fight for her to stay in my life though. "Besides, maybe we end up together anyway. I wouldn't be opposed to that."

"Me either." She smiled.

I kissed her lips softly. I couldn't resist her. Everything about her was connected to me.

"I could still end up like her," she said.

I nodded. I'd thought about that, too. About all the things that have happened to us, and I know that if she did, we could handle it. "I won't leave you. I'll always be your best friend and anything you let me be."

"I know."

"You're already pretty crazy. What's a little more?" I said, trying to lighten the mood. It didn't work.

"We never know when a day will be good or bad."

"I never know that now," I said.

She shook her head. "You're ridiculous."

"We both know this won't be easy," I said. She knew what I meant—leaving her, leaving us. Being Graham without Cassie but with her all the same. "We did it once before; we can do it again."

She rested her head on my shoulder. "Some days are torturous, horrible, no good days."

"I know it will be okay. We all have good days. We all have bad days. On the bad ones, I'll remember the good things. Days like this. Moments like this."

"Like this?"

She kissed me softly.

"And this?" She kissed me again, wrapping her arms around my neck. This time, it was longer, and God, it really was some kind of torture and I hadn't left her yet.

"Exactly," I said.

60.

Cassie

GRAHAM'S PARENTS FLEW outside like they were on fire. They were always like that. Mr. Tucker wasn't a hugger, but he shook my hand and tossed Graham's last bag in the truck.

"Good luck, Cassie, honey. Timothy said to call him when you get there," Mrs. Tucker said, swooping me up in a hug. She'd made all these plans that Graham's brother would show me around. It was sweet, really.

"Have a nice drive," I said.

She waved at me then yelled: "George, did you get the GPS?"

"I got it. I got it!" he called back. "Come on, son. Let's go!"

The doors slammed around us and they disappeared inside the cars. Graham and I looked at each other one more time. He hugged me again, pressing a kiss onto my temple, and then he let me go and went toward the car. I wasn't going to cry. I would see him tomorrow.

I turned back to go to my house, but tomorrow suddenly felt like forever. Like too long.

Tomorrow would feel like nothing for someone who was just a friend.

That wasn't Graham. I didn't want it to be.

I ran.

Graham's truck was only two blocks away, just past the stop sign. I could make it. But then it went, and I yelled Graham's name. Then the break lights came on, and I ran faster as the door opened and there he was.

"And don't forget, this," I said. I pressed my mouth against his, and his fingers burned into my back. I couldn't get close enough to him. My brain was spinning, my body aching, and somewhere in that kiss the tears escaped my eyes. I didn't let it stop me though. I relished in our kiss, in the heat between us and the emotion. I let it sweep me away, and when I thought I couldn't take anymore, Graham pulled away.

We stood there, foreheads together, panting. He breathed my name.

"Moments like this," he said.

I kissed him again softly and his parents honked, a few feet in front of his truck. I didn't want to let him go, but he had to go. We each had our own paths now.

"I should go," he said.

I shook my head. "Not until you say you'll be my boyfriend."

Graham's eyes widened. "What about all the hot girls waiting for me in Texas?"

He wove his fingers with mine. This was worth it. I knew that completely.

"I know it won't be easy," I said, "but I want to be with you. I'll visit, and you'll visit, and we'll have breaks and—we'll just work it out somehow. I don't want to give up on us just because of distance."

"That's the best thing I've ever heard," he said. Then he kissed me again, and I smiled under his lips.

"I love you, Graham Tucker."

"I love you," he said, as he backed away slowly and didn't take his eyes off me until he couldn't walk backward. "I'll call you when I get there." He was smiling as he got into the truck, and I stayed in the road until I couldn't see him anymore.

Back at my house, I took a seat on one of our old beat up metal chairs on the porch, and stared down the street where Graham had gone. I didn't know what would happen, but Graham was right. We would always have days like this, days layered with the perfect amount of happiness and sadness and hope. Days that were captured and frozen into a beautiful song.

Acknowledgements

THIS BOOK HAS been a labor of love for so many people, myself included. But since I can't thank myself, I'll thank everyone I can think of (and probably some that I will fail to mention!)

To Jenny Adams Perinovic who designed my book inside and out, who inspires me with friendship and never lets anything stand in her way. You were there the very first day I had the idea for this story and you've stuck with us (me and this story) for years now. I would not have had the courage to pursue publication without your support, encouragement, dedication, patience and endless guidance. Thanks for having my back as I have had yours, and I can't wait to see what we do next!

Thank you to my agent, Nicole Resciniti. She found me with this book, fell in love with Cassie and Graham, and championed the story—and me—each day. You believe in me more than I believe in myself some days, and I'm so grateful to have you in my corner, Nic!

To Patricia Riley, Lelia Nebeker, and Cindy Thomas, who are three of my best friends and cheerleaders. You three have read, re-read, loved, supported, cheered for, and cried over this book so many times. You're each part of the reason it's a real thing that everyone gets to read now. I wouldn't be able to survive daily life (and writing) without your friendship!

To Madelyn Rosenberg, Christina Ferko, Traci Inzitari and Kelly Hager for reading, loving this book and providing feedback. To my copy editor Sarah Henning and two proofers, Sydnee Thompson and Rachael Kirkendall, for going above and beyond to help make this perfect! To Rachel Harris for cheering me on.

The writing community of readers, bloggers, authors and writers has been extraordinary. I thank you for your excitement, encouragement, understanding and alcohol! You're all priceless to me.

To musicians everywhere who inspire and shape lives. I, like Cassie and so many others, find my way in life because of your stories. Never stop sharing.

This book is dedicated to my mom, who has fought harder, loved more, made mistakes, learned from them and grown more times than I can count. You're a beacon to me, even when we're malfunctioning or on different ends of something, and I always know that I can turn to you. Thank you for always letting me be own person and go the way I felt was best. Cassie and Joyce's story isn't ours, but there's so much I learned from it. I love you always.

And lastly to you, the one reading, buying, reviewing, promoting *Days Like This*. Sharing powerful stories about characters who overcome with you is the reason I write. I hope Cassie and Graham's journey resonates with you. Life is hard, love is harder, and finding the space to open yourself to both those things is the ultimate gift. And that's not fictional, not in any way.

About the Author

Danielle Ellison spent most of her childhood reading instead of learning math. It's probably the reason she can't divide without a calculator and has spent her life seeking the next adventure. It's also probably the reason she's had so many different zip codes and jobs.

Danielle is the author of the YA duology, *Salt* and *Storm,* about a snarky teenage demon-hunting witch without any magic, and of *The Boundless Trilogy*, about a girl trying to navigate a dystopian society where every piece of information leads to more lies. The first book, *Follow Me Through Darkness* is out now, and the sequel *Seek Me In Shadows*, releases October 2015. *Days Like This* is her first voyage into new adult romance.

When she's not writing, Danielle is probably eating cookies, fighting her nomadic urges, watching too much TV, or dreaming of the day when she can be British. She has settled in Northern Virginia, for now, but you can always find her on twitter @DanielleEWrites.